The Foolish
The Feckless
& The Fanatic

*Liberals and French babble
while U.S. leads battle against terrorism*

J.A. Klein

TRAFFORD

IRELAND   UNITED KINGDOM   CANADA   UNITED STATES OF AMERICA

© Copyright 2004 Joseph A. Klein. All rights reserved.

No part of this publication may be reproduced, stored in a retrieval system, or transmitted, in any form or by any means, electronic, mechanical, photocopying, recording, or otherwise, without the written prior permission of the author.

Printed in Victoria, Canada

National Library of Canada Cataloguing in Publication Data

A cataloguing record for this book that includes the U.S. Library of Congress Classification number, the Library of Congress Call number and the Dewey Decimal cataloguing code is available from the National Library of Canada. The complete cataloguing record can be obtained from the National Library's online database at: www.nlc-bnc.ca/amicus/index-e.html

ISBN 1-4120-2333-5

This book was published on-demand in cooperation with Trafford Publishing. On-demand publishing is a unique process and service of making a book available for retail sale to the public taking advantage of on-demand manufacturing and Internet marketing. On-demand publishing includes promotions, retail sales, manufacturing, order fulfilment, accounting and collecting royalties on behalf of the author.

Suite 6E, 2333 Government St., Victoria, B.C. V8T 4P4, CANADA
Phone   250-383-6864   Toll-free 1-888-232-4444 (Canada & US)
Fax   250-383-6804   E-mail   sales@trafford.com
Web site   www.trafford.com   TRAFFORD PUBLISHING IS A DIVISION OF TRAFFORD
                                HOLDINGS LTD.
Trafford Catalogue #04-0161   www.trafford.com/robots/04-0161.html

10   9   8   7   6   5   4   3

TABLE OF CONTENTS

CHAPTER ONE
    BLIND EYE TO EVIL 1

CHAPTER TWO
    TEN MYTHS OF THE FOOLISH AND FECKLESS 20

    Myth #1

    Islamic terrorism is the West's fault, which we can only eliminate by understanding the causes and negotiating a solution. Muslim youth turn to violence as a desperate response to Israel's occupation of the Palestinian lands and Western oppression of the Arab poor.

    Myth #2

    President Bush ignored prior warnings and a plan from the Clinton Administration to combat Al Qaeda that could have prevented September 11th.

    Myth #3

    There is nothing linking Saddam Hussein's Iraqi regime to Al Qaeda.

    Myth #4

    The French were acting with the best moral intentions as our good friends by trying to pursue a peaceful resolution of the Iraqi conflict and helping us avoid war at all cost.

Myth #5

The Iraqi war violated the United Nations Charter. It was an illegal use of force because it was not approved by the Security Council, which has the "sole" authority to declare war against a sovereign nation.

Myth #6

President Bush knew all along that there were no weapons of mass destruction (WMD) in Iraq. He deliberately lied to the American people to justify his aggressive war plans.

Myth #7

The Iraqi war was illegitimate because it was all about oil.

Myth #8

Concentration on Iraq has undermined the "war on terror".

Myth #9

The Bush Administration is assaulting our civil liberties in the name of terrorism prevention.

Myth #10

"Liberals love America like grown-ups" (Al Franken). George Bush is a cowboy who is out of his depth.

CHAPTER THREE
    FRENCH FRUSTRATION 66

CHAPTER FOUR
    PEARL HARBOR REDUX 71

CHAPTER FIVE
    FINAL THOUGHTS 75

1

BLIND EYE TO EVIL

> "The only thing necessary
> for the triumph of evil
> is for good men to do nothing."
> (*Edmund Burke*)

Or for selfish people to obstruct those who are trying to do the right thing.

And so it is today as the feckless French and foolish liberals turn a blind eye to the face of sheer evil.

It is not that these lost souls want the fanatical enemy to win. I give the liberals and French credit for not being suicidal. But they are so wrapped up in their own agendas that they cannot see anything beyond themselves. Both the liberals and French distrust American power more than they seem to fear the global terrorist threat.

This book takes a hard look at the fallacies and motivations that drive this irrational thinking. What is it about the mentality of the megalomaniac enemy we are facing that the foolish liberals and feckless French don't seem to get? Why are they unable or unwilling to connect the dots between the fanatic Islamist terrorists and a rogue tyrant like Saddam Hussein who have used each other to satiate their common fury against everything that America stands for and to fulfill their murderous impulses to bring us to reckoning? This book connects the dots in the war on terror that the opponents of President Bush's policies in Iraq refuse to see.

The Islamist fanatics' end game is simple enough. They want to destroy our way of life to expiate the humiliation of Western influence that they imagine has "defiled" Islam. The fanatics see our very success as a mortal threat to their own perverted version of the "pure" Islam world over which they thirst to rule. The fact that their nihilist version has very little to do with the real teachings of the Koran does not stop these fanatical leaders from killing all who are the villains of their delusions. This even includes the massacre of other Muslims who the fanatics believe have been "tainted" by or susceptible to Western influence, as witnessed by the wanton killings of scores of Shiites in Iraq and Pakistan on their holiest day of the Shiite calendar.

Saddam Hussein lived off the fantasies of his omnipotent power in the Arab world - the leader who dared to take on the United States. He doubled his efforts after his humiliating defeat in the first Persian Gulf conflict to get back at the Great Satan. Saddam, the secularist, and bin Laden, the Sunni fanatic, shared an abiding hatred of the United States. Their coordinated activities are well-documented, as we shall see in Chapter 2. For the record, here is a sampling of the sentiments of Saddam Hussein and his state-controlled press concerning 9/11, and their musings on even more catastrophic attacks to come:

> *"The United States reaps the thorns its rulers have planted in the world."* Saddam Hussein, September 12, 2001

> *"[I]t is possible to turn to biological attack, where a small can, not bigger than the size of a hand, can be used to release viruses that affect everything..."* Babil, September 20, 2001 (State-controlled newspaper)

> *"The United States must get a taste of its own poison..."* Babil, October 8, 2001

> *"If the attacks of September 11 cost the lives of 3,000 civilians, how much will the size of losses in 50 states within 100 cities if it were attacked in the same way in which New York and Washington were? What would happen if hundreds of planes attacked American cities?"* Al-Rafidayn, September 11, 2002 (State-controlled newspaper)

The countries of Eastern and Central Europe connected the dots between the terrorist fanatics and their state sponsors, and they understood the perils to freedom and global security that an aggressive despot like Saddam Hussein posed. They dared to confront the French with the truth, borne out by their own experience with tyranny. But President Jacques Chirac of France told the Central and Eastern European countries to keep their views on Iraq to themselves or risk losing their chance to join the European Union. "We thought we were preparing for war with Saddam Hussein and not Jacques Chirac," said Alexandr Vondra, deputy foreign minister of the Czech Republic (*Source: The New York Times, February 18, 2003*).

French President Chirac - featured on this book's front cover – is obsessed with cutting the United States down to size. He has used the term "contrepoids," or counterweight, to describe Europe – led by France, of course - as a balancing force against the world's only remaining superpower. As this book will explain in greater detail, President George W. Bush's assertive leadership has been Chirac's worst nightmare.

"There is no alternative but the United Nations," Chirac declared in a speech to the U.N. in September 2003. Chirac said that President Bush's decision to use military force to bring down Saddam Hussein's regime without final Security Council approval "shook the multilateral system" and that "(T)he United Nations has just been through one of the most grave crises in its history." What he really should have said was that his own pouting at a decisive moment in history and threats to veto decisive action by the Security Council to enforce its own resolutions against Saddam Hussein sabotaged efforts to win majority support in the United Nations for war on Iraq and ultimately rendered France even more irrelevant than it already was.

The liberals love to whine and complain when they confront a decisive leader who demonstrates moral clarity. This book uses Al Gore as a leading example of the liberals' confusion of priorities, their amnesia concerning their own former positions on the Iraqi threat and their naive over-reliance on multilateralism as a solution to all the world's ills. While Gore himself is a has-been on the political scene, liberals still look to him as a folk hero and he accommodates them with his self-righteous bromides. Gore continues to spew non-stop venom at President Bush for having the courage to actually follow through on the Clinton-Gore Administration's blustering about the al Qaeda terrorists and Saddam Hussein.

But Gore is by no means alone. Indeed, Senator John Kerry, the presumptive Democratic Presidential nominee, is following in Gore's footsteps and is his natural heir to the liberal throne. For this, Kerry deserves a place on this book's front cover. Kerry is an angry man – always barking at someone or something. And Kerry has never really outgrown his habit of firing off accusatory rhetoric without any foundation in fact. More than thirty years ago he accused the United States government, his military superiors and his fellow veterans of committing war crimes and systematic atrocities in Vietnam. Today, Kerry accuses the Bush Administration and its supporters of being "the most crooked… lying group I've ever seen". Kerry has not changed the tone of his reckless charges directed at his own countrymen, apparently forgetting the pathological crimes of the real enemies we are facing today—the fanatic Islamists and their despotic state sponsors.

Like the French whose moral relativism they so emulate, the liberals are equally distrustful of what Senator Kerry referred to as "the preeminence of American power"—or "imperial" power in Kerry's lexicon when we decide to use it ourselves in our own national security interest without "international sanction" (*Address to the Council on Foreign Relations by John Kerry, December 3, 2003*).

In plain English, despite his tough talk about U.S. sovereignty over its own military, Kerry wants United Nations approval before he would take any offensive military action with U.S. troops. This theme is perfectly consistent in spirit with Kerry's declaration during his first run for Congress back in 1970 that U.S. troops should be dispersed solely under United Nations directive. Turning around President Theodore Roosevelt's famous line that the United States should walk softly and carry a big stick, Kerry would talk loudly and carry the United Nations' baggage.

Is it any wonder that the French perceive John Kerry "with so much sympathy"? (*Source: Op Ed Article in The Wall Street Journal, March 9, 2004, by Jean-Marie Colombani, editor of Le Monde*). The feckless French want to see Kerry elected because he thinks so much like them and will make the French feel important again.

And is it a surprise that Kerry brags about how unnamed foreign leaders want to see him defeat President Bush? It seems as if Kerry is running for Mr. Popularity abroad rather than running for the Presidency of the United States. Would Kerry's admirers include Iran, where the anti-American Tehran Times published on its front page the text of an e-mail from Kerry's office describing how accommodative his foreign policy will be? (*Source: Tehran Times, February 8, 2004*).

In any event, when push came to shove the liberals preferred to leave Saddam Hussein in place rather than risk the opprobrium of world opinion for forcibly removing him, no matter what the provocation. Indeed, Kerry admitted that he could not guarantee that Saddam Hussein would now be out of power in Iraq if he had been President over the past year (*Source: The Guardian, March 10, 2004*).

The liberals were willing to bow to U.N. authority in order to dilute U.S. control over the use of its own military forces for fear that the United States might be considered an empire builder or become mired in another Vietnam quagmire. Indeed, in his speech to the Council on Foreign Relations, Senator Kerry said that as President he would treat the United Nations as "a full partner". But Kerry and his fellow liberals never considered that the present structure of the U.N. Security Council offers little potential to decisively address the intractable threats of terrorism and weapons of mass destruction as a "full partner". In their zeal to placate world opinion by insisting on the United Nations stamp of approval, the liberals overlook the fact that one irrelevant country like France is empowered to use its veto power for its own selfish reasons to unilaterally block the Security Council from even being able to decide a critical issue by majority vote. The foolish liberals never weighed in the balance the potentially catastrophic consequences if they were wrong about Saddam Hussein's intentions. Nor did they consider the example to other ambitious dictators with access to weapons of mass destruction if Saddam Hussein were allowed to flout the United Nations indefinitely with impunity.

President Bush acted only after France unilaterally made it impossible for the United Nations to enforce its own resolutions and – with a handful of other obstructionists – effectively blocked NATO from getting involved. And he acted not alone but in concert with other concerned countries – Great Britain, Spain, Italy, the Szech Republic, Poland, Japan, and Australia, for example. Unless the liberals equate multilateralism with endless consensus building, foreign polls and debate before the United States can take forceful action against enemies determined to hurt us, President Bush did nothing more than lead the world forward in the War on Terror. An endless debating society does not stop the likes of Osama bin Laden and Saddam Hussein.

Osama bin Laden, the wealthy prodigal son of a leading industrialist family in Saudi Arabia, had no religious standing of his own. Yet he took it upon himself to issue fatwas for a holy jihaad against the West. Expelled from his homeland and stateless ever since, he usurped authority illegitimately, rather than succeed to leadership by right under traditional Islam law. He exercised his authority arbitrarily in a manner that defies all principles of Islamic justice: consultation, known as shura; consensus, known as ijmaa; and independent judgment, known as ijtihad.

Bin Laden kills indiscriminately, defying Islamic law that bans killing by stealth and targeting a defenseless victim in a way intended to cause terror in a society:

> *"Do not cheat or commit treachery, nor should you mutilate or kill children, women, or old men."*

Forgetting the first principles of Islamic law, this imposter gloated in the mass killings of September 11th as the apparent fulfillment of his perverted reading of the following verse from the Koran, (Q. 4:78):

> *"Where ye are, death will find you, even if ye are in **Towers**, built up strong and tall"* (emphasis added).

Bin Laden is perfectly willing to brainwash his followers into sacrificing their lives for the illusion of eternal paradise. Not that bin Laden and his chief lieutenants are ready to die for their cause just yet. They want others to die so that they can live out their fantasies of a world converted in their image.

How does he get away with it? By skillfully preying on the weaknesses of others—

- The alienated and gullible youths who die for him.
- The wealthy Saudis who contribute their money, believing they are financing the final victory of traditional Islam over the infidels.
- The mainstream clerics, well-intentioned but cowered into silence, who let the power hungry thugs highjack Islam to use as their ideological patina for evil.
- The megalomaniac dictators like Saddam Hussein, driven by revenge against a common enemy.
- The porous borders of free nations that take in Muslim immigrants

who then turn around and drain the lifeblood of their host societies.
- The short-sighted, blinded by their greed, cowardice or folly.

Tyrants like Saddam Hussein suit the fanatic Islamists' ambitions perfectly. Imagine having an ally next door to Saudi Arabia from which al Qaeda and Saddam could launch attacks and seize the Saudi oil and the royal treasury. Money, bases, safe havens, protected training facilities and flow of arms from sponsor states are the nutrients that rootless terrorist tumor cells need to stay alive.

It is highly likely, for example, that while ensconced in Afghanistan, al Qaeda already received technical designs for nuclear bomb making from its allies in neighboring Pakistan. But technology alone is next to useless, without the means to convert it into nuclear bombs and to deliver the bombs to their intended targets. Without actual control over Pakistan, which has had an on again off again relationship with the United States for years before September 11th, al Qaeda had to hedge its bets. So it cultivated clandestine contacts with other states in the hands of enemies of the United States, such as Iraq, which had their own WMD programs and money to back them up. And Iraq would have served as a convenient base from which terrorists could launch attacks on bin Laden's homeland of Saudi Arabia—which, in addition to its oil riches and religious symbols, was believed to be in the process of acquiring nuclear weaponry of its own (*Source: Jane's Intelligence Digest, October 21 2003*).

Driven by revenge against the United States for being humiliated in the first Gulf War and for continued challenges to his ruthless ways, Saddam had every reason to enter into an unholy alliance cemented by hatred of a common enemy ("the enemy of my enemy is my friend").

Saddam's own evil knew no bounds. His genocidal use of chemical weapons against his own people and against his neighbors demonstrated that he had no compunctions about killing even his fellow Muslims. Saddam had his own terrorist organization, which he used at times to strike at his enemies including former President Bush. But Saddam wanted more than anything else to survive in power. So what better way to get revenge than subcontract the dirty work to the gullible "martyrs" recruited by the stateless al Qaeda terrorist network, who could not be traced back to Saddam?

All of this and more were staring the feckless French and foolish liberals in the face. But they turned a blind eye. At a crucial point in history, they chose a course even worse than doing nothing. They obstructed decisive action against the growing malignancy of Osama bin Laden, Saddam Hussein and their fellow psychotic killers.

In their own way and for their own selfish reasons, the French (along with other European elites) and the liberal establishment cannot abide decisive assertions of U.S. power. They want to bring the United States down to a level that is indistinguishable from any other country. In a world of moral ambivalence that the feckless French and the foolish liberals are used to inhabiting, the United States government is no less to blame for what happened on September 11th than the terrorists and dictators who support them.

It was not very long after September 11th that an astounding book of vitriol entitled "Horrifying Fraud" became a best-seller in France. Its readers were captivated by the book's libelous contention that the horrors of September 11th were not really the handiwork of any fanatical Islamist terrorists at all. It was all a conspiracy that the Pentagon concocted to justify an increase in the military budget. The book goes so far as to doubt that there was any airplane crash into the Pentagon since it did not immediately collapse from the shock of the impact. In the ultimate insult to the memory of the passengers who perished on that fateful day, the author asks: "What became of the passengers of American Airlines flight 77? Are they dead?"

Michael Moore is the darling of liberal intellectuals here in the U.S. and of French and German audiences alike. He loves the applause when he attacks his own countrymen and their leaders. Somehow, in his twisted logic, September 11th was all George Bush's fault:

> "Am I angry? You bet I am. I am an American citizen, and my leaders have taken my money to fund mass murder. And now my friends have paid the price with their lives."

Moore goes on to ask a series of accusatory questions of President Bush. Moore was especially interested in the Bush family's ties to Saudi Arabia and in particular to the bin Laden family.

Well, I have several questions for Mr. Moore:

- Why don't you save even a thimbleful of your venom for the madmen actually responsible for the murder of 3000 innocent people?
- Why did you make fun of the innocent victims on board those highjacked planes, calling them cowards for not fighting back? By the way, how brave are you when you are escorted around in your corporate limos spouting your idiocy under the watchful eyes of your hired security guards?
- Were the hijackers your heroes because they were willing to sacrifice their lives in a sick cause?
- Why do you run off to Germany of all places where you compare Bush to Hitler and tell the Germans, whose myopia made Hitler possible, how stupid you think the American people are? Are you afraid to say this in your own country to the survivors of Hitler's concentration camps and to the American soldiers who fought to rescue the German and French people from Hitler's deathtrap and who stayed to protect them against Soviet domination?
- Wasn't it American brains and money that helped the Germans figure out how to build a successful democracy and economy? By the way, Mr. Moore, how many Nobel prizes in medicine, physics or economics have the Germans or French won in the last decade compared to the United States? Maybe the answer has something to do with the fact that the United States is more educated across a broad spectrum of its population, spending twice the percentage of its gross domestic product on higher education than Europe does, according to a recent report of the European Commission. (*Source: New York Times, December 25, 2003, p. A-3*).
- If you are so concerned about friendly associations with Saudi Arabia and the bin Laden family in particular, have you lost any sleep over the fact that former President Clinton took their blood money after September 11th?
- Did you know that Clinton not only received a $267,000 speaking fee for going to Osama bin Laden's hometown of Jeddah, Saudi Arabia in January 2002 to address a forum funded in part by the bin Laden family - four short months after Saudi-born highjackers

killed 3000 innocent people - but also received a hefty pledge in the millions of dollars for his presidential library in Little Rock, Ark., according to high-ranking Saudis? (*Source: Robert Novak March 30, 2002; Arab News, Friday, 25, January, 2002 (12, Dhul Qa`dah, 1422)*)

The feckless French and foolish liberals alike bellow how our actions in Iraq changed everything for the worse. The world was with us before Iraq, they complain, and we squandered all the good will we garnered following September 11th by launching a unilateral attack upon a sovereign nation in the face of international opposition.

Lets see what was really going on. Our "friends" in France loved seeing the United States in the position of a helpless giant. In a world where the United States could not protect itself alone if need be, France could become relevant again. The last thing the French wanted to see was a resurgence of muscular leadership in the United States that took control of its own fate by bringing the war against the terrorists to their sponsoring dictators.

Twenty-five percent of the French surveyed in a poll on the Iraq war actually wanted Iraq to win, slightly less than the number favoring the U.S. side! Just over 30% said they supported neither side. (*Source: BBC News, April 1, 2003 quoting a Le Monde/TF1 poll*).

French journalists wrote about every military setback in Iraq as if the United States and its allies were suffering a resounding defeat on the order of Waterloo. Their readers were told how wrong the war was and how America was paying the price for its arrogance. Very little was said about the celebrations of the Iraqi people when the coalition's victory - with no help from France - brought them the taste of freedom.

Lest we forget, Saddam lost the first Gulf War, waged after his wanton aggression against his neighbors and genocide against his own people that not even France could ignore. We did not remove him from power back then as we should have, in deference to the opinions of our coalition partners who wanted to stick with the limited United Nations mission of kicking Saddam out of Kuwait. In other words, we played the game of multilateral consensus politics and lost big-time.

Like a paroled killer, Saddam had his chance to redeem himself. He had to show that he could obey the rules of civilized nations and give up his quest for weapons of mass destruction. In fact, he was given many chances.

Instead, since the first Gulf War ended with a shaky cease-fire, Saddam has spat repeatedly in the world's face. He flouted one United Nations resolution after another - for more than 12 years. Saddam made the decision to keep a state of war going when he shot at our planes trying to keep him from unleashing more poison gas attacks against his own people and when he refused to cooperate with the ineffectual United Nations inspectors. President Clinton bombed his military installations and threatened to remove him, all to no effect. When President Bush warned during the 2000 campaign that he would take more forceful action if necessary to bring Saddam to account, Saddam apparently took this as yet another meaningless bluff. With complete contempt for the United Nations, Saddam brazenly skimmed billions of dollars from the humanitarian oil-for-food program under the noses of U.N. monitors.

Even after Saddam was given one final chance after the unanimous passage of Security Council Resolution 1441, he played for time and relied on the French and Russians to run interference for him. The French voted for the resolution but were willing to continue the charade indefinitely. Up to the very last minute, Saddam could have lived out his life in exile and spared his country from attack. He chose defiance and finally met his fate - cornered like a rat in the hole in the ground where he was found hiding and arrested. President Bush did no more than end Saddam's undeserved parole for good.

And what do we make of the French for whom the phrase "final chance" is translated in French diplomacy to mean "un plus chance toujours" (always one more chance)? I see a combination of commercialism and cowardice towering over doing the right thing.

French President Jacques Chirac ran interference for Saddam because the two had developed a long-standing business relationship, going back to the 1970's when Chirac had helped arrange France's assistance in building a nuclear reactor in Iraq. Chirac was so cozy with the Iraq dictatorship that his unofficial media title was "Sheikh Iraq"—a nice play on his real name and descriptive of his personal leanings.

And he hasn't disappointed. By 2001, France became Iraq's largest European trading partner and had controlled over 22.5 percent of Iraq's imports. Its total trade with Iraq under the oil-for-food program has totaled $3.1 billion since 1996, according to the United Nations. Saddam and Sheikh Iraq continued to do business right up to the end. Saddam signed lucrative contracts with Chirac's business cronies at Renault, Peugeot, and Alcatel. French companies had signed contracts with Iraq that are likely linked to its military operations including refrigerated trucks that could be used as mobile laboratories for biological weapons.

But this was only the prelude to what adds up to a corrupt bargain that Sheikh Iraq struck with Saddam to protect Total Fina Elf, the giant French oil company that had been one of the largest contributors to Chirac's political party in the past and which, as a major trial concluded in France has shown, was not shy about buying the influence of major politicians to protect its commercial interests. Total Fina Elf had negotiated extensive oil contracts to develop the Majnoon and Nahr Umar oil fields in southern Iraq. Both the Majnoon and Nahr Umar fields are estimated to contain as much as 25 percent of the country's oil reserves. The two fields contain an estimated 26 billion barrels of oil - more than three times as much oil as all of Total Fina Elf's total reserves at the present time. Saddam had cancelled the $4 billion Russian Lukoil contract to make a point about what would happen to friends who disappointed him at the United Nations. Total Fina Elf did not want to be next and Chirac did not want to disappoint. So Sheikh Iraq made his bargain and stalled the U.N. with every means at this disposal, wrapping his delay tactics in the self-righteous vocabulary of international law - all in the secure belief that his efforts would be rewarded with the windfall to his benefactors at Total Fina Elf.

Or so he thought. The trouble is that Sheikh Iraq's corrupt bargain did not take account of a U.S. President who saw through the French manure and actually did what he thought was right.

As for the infamous feckless French cowardice streak, David Letterman captured it best when he quipped: *"A lot of folks are still demanding more evidence before they actually consider Iraq a threat. For example, France wants more evidence. And you know I'm thinking, the last time France wanted more evidence they rolled right through Paris with the German flag."*

I find it incredible that many of the same Europeans and liberal Democrats who so vociferously opposed Bush's action against Iraq didn't think twice about bombing Serbia with no United Nations authorization. No doubt Milosovich was a bad guy, but his war crimes paled in comparison with Saddam Hussein's and nobody has suggested that Milosovich harbored any interest in weapons of mass destruction, much less possessed any weapons that he could provide to our terrorist enemies.

If the chances were even 50-50 that the megalomaniac Saddam - who imagined himself to be a direct descendant of Mohammed - would share his weapons of mass destruction with al Qaeda to get back at his greatest enemy, is it really responsible for any President to wait until there is proof beyond a reasonable doubt? Do you wait to take decisive action until a terrorist sneaks the "smoking gun" into this country in a brief case and incinerates himself in a nuclear explosion that could kill millions of innocent people?

There are too many good people who are willing to let evil triumph by not taking the unpleasant actions needed to stop it. Some of this inertia is driven by fear of the unintended consequences of war. This is an understandable feeling, but one that has had to be overcome many times in our own history so that we could hold on to our freedoms.

Reasonable people can also legitimately disagree about the tactics of the Bush Administration in fighting the war against terror. For example, has Iraq soaked up too many resources that had to be diverted from Afghanistan and elsewhere? Do we have a viable plan for transition to Iraqi self-government and an exit plan?

But when seemingly sane people go to great lengths to distort the truth and spill more venom against President Bush than against the murderous dictator whose own people danced in the streets when he was captured, one senses that blind rage against their own irrelevance and sense of powerlessness has replaced any rational thought. Myths are created and then repeated as if they were the unassailable truth.

I dissect these myths in the next chapter. But first I want to explain why I think we are seeing so much rage and defeatism deflected at the wrong target.

Not to pick on the French but they do offer some psychological insights, beyond the corrupt motives of Sheikh Iraq.

I label the French feckless because they remind me of the aged Hollywood actress who cannot adjust to the fact that time has passed her by and so still dresses as if she were fifty years younger.

France has become a caricature of her former glorious past. She struts the world stage as if her opinions really mattered anymore. But France has contributed nothing of significance to the world of culture or to political and economic thought for many decades. Her statist and union-dominated economy continues to stagnate.

Rather than look to the future and open their society to new sources and opportunities for vibrancy that they can contribute to the world, the French would rather wallow in self-pity and establish a commission to eradicate Anglo-American influences on their culture. Rather than intellectually engage the points of view of the liberated countries of Eastern Europe, President Chirac has a temper tantrum and tells them to shut up when they dare to speak out in the defense of freedom.

France is a country whose leader looks back wistfully to its place in the sun during the Napoleonic and colonial era but can barely muster a force to quell a disturbance in one of its small former colonies in Africa. In fact, France has not won a war since Napolean's defeat at Waterloo in 1815 and was the only country of the five permanent members of the U.N. Security Council that had to be rescued from an Axis power rather than fight on the winning side.

The French have a saying - "Plus ça change, plus c'est la même chose" (The more things change, the more they stay the same). The problem is that times have really changed and will never be the same again for the French. They cannot accept their inferior role to the United States. They cannot accept the fact that they no longer have any impact on history.

In the words of a leading French economist and lawyer, Nicolas Baverez:

> *"Overtaken by the democratic vitality and technological advance of the United State, downgraded industrially and challenged commercially by China and Asia, the decline of France is accelerating at the same rhythm as the vast changes in the world."* (From "La France Qui Tombe," by Nicolas Baverez as quoted in the International Herald Tribune, October 2, 2003)

France's marginalization drives the French mad. And so they try to contain the United States whenever and however they can, even if in doing so they are hurting themselves in the long run. I will have more to say about the French and their strategies for weakening the United States in Chapter 3.

The foolish liberals have their own psychological reasons for the myths they spout. David Frum, in his review of Al Franken's *Lies and the Lying Liars Who Tell Them: A Fair and Balanced Look at the Right*, wrote that Al

Franken was an example of a liberal-left Democrat who eschews self-criticism, is not interested in any real discussion of ideas and can only lash out against "unbelievers' as the cause of the liberals' own failures. Frum compares this mentality to that of the fanatic Islamists themselves.

That's a little harsh, but Franken should not care. As he keeps telling himself through his alter ego Saturday Night Live character Stuart Smalley, "I'm good enough, I'm smart enough, and dog-gone it, people like me." The Clintons love the guy. That's because Franken's idea of "fair and balanced" is to have Bill Clinton whispering what Franken should say in his right ear and Hillary Rodham Clinton whispering what to say in his left ear.

Liberals like Franken and Moore have serious psychological problems dealing with strong authority figures. They are still in their rebellious adolescence phase, attacking authority while hiding behind it for protection - a case of arrested development. They are afraid to confront real evil in the world with the force needed to defeat it. So instead they make up demons of their own to attack, like President Bush, Rush Limbaugh and Bill O'Reilly. Afraid to confront their ideological opponents in an actual debate of ideas, the foolish liberals prefer to lob their rhetorical bombs from a safe distance. And in the process, liberals have lost all perspective, not to mention their moral bearings.

Thus, you have a former Democratic contender for President, Howard Dean, repeating slanderous nonsense - picked up by his liberal supporters - that President Bush was warned in advance about what was going to happen on September 11th. At the same time, Dean was more willing to give bin Laden the benefit of the doubt. In his own words, Dean would not "prejudge jury trials" with regard to determining whether Osama bin Laden was guilty of the September 11th attacks - this incredible suspension of judgment despite bin Laden's own admission of complicity (*Source: Concord Monitor Online, December 26, 2003*):

> *The Monitor asked: Where should Osama bin Laden be tried if he's caught? Dean said he didn't think it made any difference, and if he were president he would consult with his lawyers for advice on the subject.*
>
> *But wouldn't most Americans feel strongly that bin Laden should be tried in America - and put to death?*

> *"I've resisted pronouncing a sentence before guilt is found," Dean said. "I still have this old-fashioned notion that even with people like Osama, who is very likely to be found guilty, we should do our best not to, in positions of executive power, not to prejudge jury trials. So I'm sure that is the correct sentiment of most Americans, but I do think if you're running for president, or if you are president, it's best to say that the full range of penalties should be available. But it's not so great to prejudge the judicial system."*

And in a classic of example of putting one's foot even deeper down one's mouth, Dean tried to clarify his position on bin Laden the next day by telling the Associated Press that "As a president, I would have to defend the rule of law. But as an American, I want to make sure he gets the death penalty he deserves."

Dean will not be the next President, thank goodness, but his confusion over how to apply our rule of law to the foreign Islamist terrorists we capture is typical of many liberals. The short answer is that they do not get any of the protections when they are caught committing or conspiring in acts of war against us. As Commander-in-Chief, the President of the United States really does not have to worry about providing bin Laden an attorney to defend himself.

Maybe a tough bird like Judge Judy would give bin Laden the sentence he deserves, but I for one do not want to take the chance. Ordinary "rule of law" with jury trials and endless Court appeals don't apply to someone who has declared war on us and has begun to carry it out. In the words of a former Supreme Court judge, "the Constitution is not a suicide pact." We would be crazy to hand bin Laden our precious tools of Constitutional protections for him to turn around and use them as weapons to destroy us. I think that we will all be much safer with President Bush's pre-emptive action in the battlefield than with the liberals' penchant for giving terrorists a day in court.

And why do feminists constantly attack President Bush on women's rights issues, but make no speeches denouncing Saddam Hussein for his regime's atrocities against women, including rampant rape and torture. This was a man who, in an attempt to garner support from Islamists, had female dissidents stoned to death on trumped up charges of adultery. That alone should be reason enough for any feminists with their heads on straight to at least shut up about the war. But some feminists win the Fool of the Year award by actually denouncing the war to remove Saddam as a step backwards for the women's movement! (*See Wall Street Journal, The Women Feminists Forgot, March 7, 2003 by Kay S. Hymowitz*).

It is usually best to let the fools speak for themselves, since trying to summarize their nonsense does not do them justice. These are the words of NOW Action Vice President Olga Vives, speaking about NOW's opposition to a war on Iraq at a news conference on Oct. 10, 2002, the eve of the congressional vote on whether to take military action:

> *"We know that women would be disproportionately affected if Congress gives Bush a blank check to invade Iraq with a unilateral, preemptive strike. As has happened during previous wars, funds will be diverted from education, health, welfare and other vitally needed social programs from an already downsized budget. Women will bear the greatest burden of any decrease in domestic spending in order to finance war.*
>
> ***For Iraqi women, the war carries the danger that their nation will degenerate into an even more militarized society. We know all too well how such an extreme militarized culture in Afghanistan gave rise to a life of violence and oppression for women there. A U.S. invasion of Iraq will likely entail similar dangers to the safety and rights of Iraqi women—who currently enjoy more rights and freedoms than women in other Gulf nations, such as Saudi Arabia…*** (emphasis added)*"*

I guess Iraqi and Afghan women should just let the advocates of women's rights concentrate their energies on fighting for things that really matter to them, like partial birth abortion. Maybe it is just a coincidence that the proponents of partial birth abortion are as willing to ignore the suffering experienced by near-born infants during late-term abortions as they are willing to tolerate Saddam's violence against his women subjects. After all, they blame Bush for trying to end both forms of brutality.

Liberals take freedom for granted, never absorbing the lessons of history that evil forces left unchecked will threaten the very foundation of freedom.

Forgetting that the United States military was an instrument for good in vanquishing the totalitarian evils of Nazism and Communism without keeping any spoils of war for itself, the liberals believe that the U.S. is more dangerous than any other country today because we have the military power to impose our will. They do not differentiate why or how military force is used. In their world, Saddam's Iraq and the United States are both on the same moral plane, each with its own imperialistic designs.

But what would have been the outcome if Saddam got his way with the use of force? More mass graves for his own people? Another invasion of Kuwait, Iran, Saudi Arabia or other neighboring countries? Would the oil coming under his control be used to pay for more schools, electricity, hospitals, and better housing for his people or for completing his program of weapons of mass destruction that nobody seriously denies was his greatest ambition?

And what is the United States' track record when it comes to occupation of conquered lands? Yes, there was allied rule for four years in Germany and for seven years in Japan. There are American troops remaining in both places today. But can anyone seriously deny that, as a result of all this, the two countries have become paragons of liberal democracy, their people are far better off and they no longer pose any military threat to their neighbors? Does the use of military force that ends a brutal dictatorship and begins an opportunity for human dignity and freedom have no better moral standing to liberals than the use of military force to do the very opposite? Apparently, in the liberal mind, military force is an evil in itself, no matter what its reason or its outcome, unless sanctioned by "international law" and "consensus" of the world community.

The liberals are fools because they naively believe that international law is a talisman that can solve every problem if only we keep working at it. But a legal and political system only works when all under its jurisdiction share a common set of values and willingness to enforce its rules if necessary. Where there is no accountability, endless debate and deception become the tactic of some to forestall the action necessary to secure a true basis for peace under law.

The fanatic Islamists make no bones about acting entirely outside this system. Their goal is to destroy the system by whatever means necessary, and they have declared war against the United States. The liberals are foolish enough to believe that weak multilateral institutions, treaties and cease-fires that are disrespected by tyrants like Saddam Hussein are sufficient to protect the civilized world against the mortal harm threatened by the fanatics and their state sponsors. The liberals simply do not trust their own government's ability to use credible military force for good, irrespective of America's sacrifices in two World Wars and the Cold War.

Neither the feckless French nor the foolish liberals can accept the truth of what President Bush actually accomplished or how he did it.

- He challenged the United Nations to enforce its own resolutions.

- He gave them ample time and opportunity to meet their obligation to use collective force under the U.N. Charter when all lesser measures have been repeatedly tried and failed.

- He negotiated in good faith with the other members of the Security Council to this end, but set realistic deadlines which he was willing to extend several times.

- In the end President Bush kept his word that he would not forfeit his responsibility to the American people to confront evil directly whenever necessary to protect our freedoms.

- President Bush told us what he was going to do, followed through with what he promised and did what was right rather than what was expedient. This is obviously foreign to those used to Clintonian and French doublespeak, so Bush's opponents make up the myths that we discuss in the next chapter.

2

TEN MYTHS OF THE FOOLISH AND FECKLESS

Myth #1 - Islamic terrorism is the West's fault, which we can only eliminate by understanding the causes and negotiating a solution. Muslim youth turn to violence as a desperate response to Israel's occupation of the Palestinian lands and Western oppression of the Arab poor.

Those who truly believe this nonsense should rent the movie "Independence Day", which was a sensational hit back in 1996. When the President of the United States confronted one of the alien creatures who had been captured during their invasion of Earth and asked him "What do you want us to do?," the alien replies simply, "Die!" Only then did the President give up any pretense that the aliens could be reached by negotiation and reason.

At least twice - in 1996 and 1998 - bin Laden issued declarations of war against the United States in so-called fatwas.

He left little to the imagination: *"The ruling to kill the Americans and their allies—civilians and military—is an individual duty for every Muslim who can do it in any country in which it is possible to do it"* (Jihad Against Jews and Crusaders World Islamic Front Statement 23 February 1998)

In a letter from Osama bin Laden to the People of America printed in the Observer on November 24, 2002, his answer was just as chilling -

"What are we calling you to, and what do we want from you?
(1) The first thing that we are calling you to is Islam"

By which he means his twisted and maniacal version of Islam. In other words, his message to us was as direct and final as the alien in "Independence Day" - to give up our way of life or be prepared to die in the name of Allah. September 11th was merely his calling card.

Al Franken says he hates the terrorists and even goes so far as to admit that what they did was "horrific and inexcusable." But he wants to understand what triggered the terrorists' violence. How about if he did something shocking for a change, like reading bin Laden's words for himself?

Fanatics have a way of signaling their own evil designs with plenty of advance notice. The problem is that the right people do not pay enough attention. Hitler wrote his Mein Kampf, which he started when he was imprisoned during the 1920's. It was his blueprint for world domination, but nobody took it seriously until it was too late. Maybe the French could have saved us all a lot of grief if they had prepared wisely against Hitler's call for France's destruction. They had more than fifteen years to do so, but waited until it was too late. As we will see, President Clinton was going down the same road of "benign neglect." It takes courage to confront evil as directly as it confronts you. The French had their warning. We have ours. The difference is that we are finally taking the threat against us seriously, while the French ignored the following warning from Hitler:

As long as the eternal conflict between Germany and France is carried on only in the form of a German defense against French aggression, it will never be decided, but from year to year, from century to century, Germany will lose one position after another. Follow the movements of the German language frontier beginning with the twelfth century until today, and you will hardly be able to count on the success of an attitude and a development which has done us so much damage up till now. Only when this is fully understood in Germany, so that the vital will of the German nation is no longer allowed to languish in purely passive defense, but is pulled together for a final active reckoning with France and thrown into a last decisive struggle with the greatest ultimate aims on the German side- only then will we be able to end the eternal and essentially so fruitless struggle between ourselves and France; presupposing, of course, that Germany actually regards the destruction of France as only a means which will afterward enable her finally to give our people the expansion made possible elsewhere (Volume Two- A Reckoning, Chapter XV: The Right of Emergency Defense).

Bin Laden was no less subtle in signaling his intentions. He had already given us a taste of what was in store, with the first World Trade Center attack, even before his long rambling fatwa, or declaration of war, was published in Al Quds Al Arabi, a London-based newspaper, in August, 1996. Here are just a few insights of what bin Laden was prepared to do, quoted from his fatwa, entitled "Declaration of War against the Americans Occupying the Land of the Two Holy Places":

"Death is truth and ultimate destiny, and life will end any way. If I do not fight you, then my mother must be insane…

"Those youths know that their rewards in fighting you, the USA, is double than their rewards in fighting some one else not from the people of the book. They have no intention except to enter paradise by killing you. An infidel, and enemy of God like you, cannot be in the same hell with his righteous executioner…

These youths know that: if one is not to be killed one will die (any way) and the most honourable death is to be killed in the way of Allah. They are even more determined after the martyrdom of the four heroes who bombed the Americans in Riyadh. Those youths who raised high the head of the Ummah and humiliated the Americans-the occupier- by their operation in Riyadh."

Bin Laden has issued a call to arms to his legions of gullible and disaffected Muslim youth. Follow him in his final battle against the infidels, Bin Laden says, and return to Islam's glory days when Islam was spread through force under the banner of revolution to become the dominating presence in much of the civilized world.

In its ascendancy, Islamic economic and military power provided fertile soil for the flowering of cultural advances in art, architecture and mathematics. Muslim leaders could afford to be tolerant to non-Muslim groups living in their midst who posed no threat. Indeed, Jews flourished in Turkey and they prospered in Spain while it was in Moorish hands. It was the Christians, not the Muslims, who tortured and expelled the Jews when the Christians assumed control.

But not even the strongest empire can survive if it does not adapt to inevitable change. The West embraced technological change and the advantages it afforded to commercial success and adapted with new political and economic structures that broke the stranglehold of religious coercion and divine monarchy. Though interrupted by paroxysms of violence and ideological "isms' of its own, the West did modernize with a political and economic combination of democratic capitalism that released individual creative energies. Much of the Muslim world remained frozen in time - tribal, theocratic, inward looking and ruled by some form of autocracy.

Failure bred humiliation which bred the contempt and hatred of the "unbelievers". Religious fundamentalism was revived with a vengeance and the Muslim world's ills were blamed on the corrupt influence of the infidels. Hatred metastasized to today's terror cells. In Osama's words in his fatwa: *"Death is better than life in humiliation! Some scandals and shames will never be otherwise eradicated."*

Bin Laden cites Zionist occupation of the Muslim holy lands, particularly Jerusalem. The truth is, however, that there could have been two states living side by side in peace for the last 45 years under the protection of the United Nations if the Arab neighbors had permitted it. Palestinians left their own homes at the urging of their Arab brothers who promised an early return after the Jewish invaders were swept into the sea. Even after Israel's triumph in the 1948 war, the Palestinians could have returned to their homes, including Jerusalem which remained in Arab hands. Israel did not occupy Jerusalem or the populations of the West Bank or the Gaza strip between 1948 and 1968. Jordan - an Arab country with a Palestinian majority of its own - controlled the West Bank and could determine its fate. Jordan was in complete control of the Muslim holy places, while excluding Jews from their holy site at the Western Wall. The Arabs preferred the Palestinian refugees to remain in homeless squalor as a way of keeping a holy war alive and diverting their own people away from their real troubles at home. The Arabs chose to use the West Bank as a launching pad for another invasion of Israel in 1967, which led Israel to retain control of this land for security reasons. Even now, however, the mosques in Jerusalem remain in Muslim control.

The truth is that bin Laden uses the Palestinians but has no real interest in a Palestinian state, according to an expert on the subject - Olivier Roy, senior researcher at the National Center for Scientific Research in Paris and the author of numerous books, including The Failure of Political Islam and The New Central Asia: The Creation of Nations:

> *"He has been critical of the Palestinians, saying, 'What use is it to create a Palestinian state? If you create a Palestinian state, it will be like many other states. You should try to mobilize the umma, the Muslim community, for your cause, but not for creating a Palestinian state.' He is opposed to the idea of a Palestinian state. Bin Laden is a man who wants to unify all the Muslim population in the world against the world power, the United States of America. He doesn't care about Palestine."* (Source: Conversation with Oliver Roy, April 16, 2002, part of U.C. Berkley's Conversation with History series of the Institute of International Studies.)

Bin Laden also demanded that the American "Crusaders" leave the holy lands of the Saudi Arabian peninsula. He exhorted his followers with words like these in his fatwa:

> *"It should not be hidden from you that the people of Islam had suffered from aggression, iniquity and injustice imposed on them by the Zionist-Crusaders alliance and their collaborators; to the extent that the Muslims blood became the cheapest and their wealth as loot in the hands of the enemies. Their blood was spilled in Palestine and Iraq...*
>
> *"The latest and the greatest of these aggressions, incurred by the Muslims since the death of the Prophet (ALLAH'S BLESSING AND SALUTATIONS ON HIM) is the occupation of the land of the two Holy Places -the foundation of the house of Islam, the place of the revelation, the source of the message and the place of the noble Ka'ba, the Qiblah of all Muslims- by the armies of the American Crusaders and their allies. (We bemoan this and can only say: "No power and power acquiring except through Allah")."*

In Bin Laden's mind, terrorism - the deliberate killing of innocent men, women and children to intimidate his enemy - is morally justified in its own right (*"Terrorising you, while you are carrying arms on our land, is a legitimate and morally demanded duty."*) Even as the fanatic Islamists have gotten their wish and American troops have moved out of Saudi Arabia as a direct result of neutralizing Saddam's threat to his Muslim neighbors, the terrorists continue to slaughter innocent Muslims in suicide attacks and they plot to assassinate Saudi Arabia's leaders. Do they really need to do this to protect their holy sites from the Western "Crusaders" who have left anyway? Or are we seeing another chapter in bin Laden's war to take control of the key stranglehold to world economic health - oil - and to get his hands on the Saudi royal treasury and possible nuclear weaponry that the royal family has begun to acquire?

And how does the Israeli-Palestinian conflict or American forces in Saudia Arabia explain the fanatics' brutal assaults on "non-believers" in far removed places like India and the Philippines? How does it justify the horrors perpetrated against their own people, like the massacres of women by Islamist extremists in Algeria? As reported in the local Algerian press on March 21, 1998, for example:

> *"Algerian sources said that more than 4,000 women were killed in attacks in Algeria, including in massacres of civilians, during the last six years. The sources said most of the women were murdered in attacks by Islamist extremists. Another 500 women were kidnapped and 300 women were raped in attacks on villages."*

Reason doesn't work with a madman like Osama bin Laden, intent on refashioning the world in his own twisted image. Until he achieves complete victory over infidels of "the House of War" - the world inhabited by non-believers - he will wage war with the blood of his youthful followers who are willing to be martyrs to his cause. Better to be dead than be humiliated he tells them - as long as you take as many of your enemies with you.

> *"These youths believe in what has been told by Allah and His messenger (Allah's Blessings and Salutations may be on him) about the greatness of the reward for the Mujahideen and Martyrs; Allah, the most exalted said: {and -so far- those who are slain in the way of Allah, He will by no means allow their deeds to perish. He will guide them and improve their condition. and cause them to enter he garden -paradise- which He has made known to them}. "*

Bin Laden and his followers have declared war on the United States and have committed heinous attacks on innocent people to back up their words. Human life means nothing to them. As bin Laden said about his followers: *"These youths love death as you loves (sic) life."*

So to Al Franken and his friends, I have this to say - I don't want to understand the terrorists. I just want them dead or put away for life.

Myth #2 - President Bush ignored prior warnings and a plan from the Clinton Administration to combat Al Qaeda that could have prevented September 11th.

It is absurd to blame anyone for the heinous attack on September 11th except for the murderers who perpetrated it. But Clinton court jesters like Al Franken (author of such learned treatises as *Lies and the Lying Liars Who Tell Them: A Fair and Balanced Look at the Right*) insist on trying to re-write history to protect the legacy of their hero. Not "Truth to power, baby" as he declares. More like self-delusion to stupidity.

Does Mr. Franken believe that the authors of the recently released Intelligence Committee report on 9-11 were lying when they concluded that his hero's Administration had received warnings of al Qaeda attacks using airliners?

> "In September 1998, the [Intelligence Community] obtained information that Bin Laden's next operation might involve flying an explosive-laden aircraft into a U.S. airport and detonating it.

> "In the fall of 1998, the [Intelligence Community] obtained information concerning a Bin Laden plot involving aircraft in the New York and Washington, D.C., areas."

> "In March 2000, the [Intelligence Community] obtained information regarding the types of targets that operatives of Bin Laden's network might strike. The Statue of Liberty was specifically mentioned, as were skyscrapers, ports, airports, and nuclear power plans."

What did the Clinton Administration do with those warnings? Absolutely nothing.

Even worse, Al Franken and his fellow Clinton worshippers deny that Sudan offered to hand over Osama bin Laden on a silver platter back in 1996 - the same year that Osama issued his first declaration of war on America. Clinton chose not to take him. Clinton the lawyer, who had his own problems with the criminal justice system, did not think there was enough evidence to convict Bin Laden of anything in a U.S. court.

Despite the first attack on the World Trade Center and escalating acts of terrorism thereafter, and despite bin Laden's declaration of war on the United States, Clinton regarded this fanatic and his followers as lawbreakers rather than public enemies who had waged war on the United States. So Clinton turned his cheek and let bin Laden slip away to Afghanistan where he and his followers metastasized. The Clinton Administration continued to spurn Sudan's offers to share crucial intelligence information that it had gathered on Osama and his followers during their sojourn in Sudan.

Franken's tactic for avoiding this painful truth is to attack the messenger. He goes after Sean Hannity, the conservative commentator, for making the Sudanese charge on his TV and radio shows and attacks the source, Mansoor Ijaz, as an unreliable friend of the Sudanese who had "a huge stake in Sudanese oil."

Franken should have told his fourteen Harvard research assistants to do a more thorough research job before he so cavalierly dismissed Ijaz's first hand account. The researchers might have told Franken that Mansoor Ijaz, an American Muslim of Pakistani origin, was actually a Clinton supporter who had contributed to Clinton's campaign. Or maybe Franken knew this but could not stomach a former Clinton ally turning on his hero with the truth.

The researchers might have also discovered that Timothy Carney, U.S. ambassador to Sudan from August 1995 to November 1997, co-wrote an article with Ijaz in The Washington Post, June 30, 2002, entitled *Intelligence Failure? Let's Go Back to Sudan*. The article recounted how the Clinton Administration had mistakenly turned down Sudan's repeated offers of vital information about al Qaeda's key operatives and financial interests in many parts of the globe. Carney, the U.S. chief diplomat in Sudan who was there at the time, put his name on the record to sadly conclude:

> "We're still living with the consequences of the U.S. policy and intelligence failure in Sudan. Khartoum offered us the best chance to engage radical Islamists and stop bin Laden early. If the United States is to account for the failures that led to the attacks of Sept. 11, we need to better understand our failures in Sudan. Solid intelligence that informs sound policy can produce the judiciousness that helps differentiate America from those who seek to destroy it."

Was Ambassador Carney a turncoat too, in Franken's eyes?

And if this still isn't enough for Al Franken, here is what Clinton himself was recorded having to say in February 2002 before the Long Island Association about his lost opportunity to nab bin Laden: *"At the time, 1996, he had committed no crime against America so I did not bring him here because we had no basis on which to hold him, though we knew he wanted to commit crimes against America."* (Source: NewsMax.com, July 7, 2002).

After the bombings of the US embassies in Kenya and Tanzania, Clinton sent a few cruise missiles to Afghanistan and managed to hit an empty pharmaceutical factory in Sudan of all places. Clinton did nothing at all after the bombing of the USS Cole in Aden, Yemen in the year 2000.

Al Qaeda took due notice of this inaction and stepped up their own offensive.

Unfortunately, Clinton's myopia did not stop there. After more terrorist incidents and a second declaration of war against America issued by the fanatical Islamists, we actually found ourselves on the side of the terrorists in Kosovo through the link of the Kosovo Liberation Army ("KLA"), sharing the common objective of helping fight off Serbian oppression of that province. The Clinton Administration simply ignored al Qaeda´s Balkan links and helped them grow. Somehow Al Franken missed this part of the story in his own version of a 'fair and balanced' rendering of the Clinton record against terrorism.

As detailed in an article from The Wall Street Journal Europe, by Marcia Christoff Kurop dated November 1, 2001, the Balkans served as a fertile recruiting and training center for al Qaeda. The cancer cells fed off the region's poverty, alienation of disaffected youth and chaos from years of conflict in Bosnia and Kosovo. Bin Laden and his lieutenants visited the Balkans multiple times over the last decade. Bin Laden's second-in-command, Ayman Al-Zawahiri, ran training camps, weapons factories and money laundering operations throughout Albania, Kosovo, Bosnia and other territories in the region. The money laundering included funneling of al Qaeda drug money and funds ostensibly raised for humanitarian purposes through front banks operating in the region. The war for "liberation" in Kosovo even received the highest status conferred by the fanatics at an international Islamic conference in Pakistan - a "jihad".

In spite of all this, and the branding of the KLA as Islamic terrorists by our own special envoy to Bosnia, the Clinton Administration continued to provide the KLA with arms and other support.

As Ms. Kurop concluded:

> *"With the future status of Kosovo still in question, the only real development that may be said to be taking place there is the rise of Wahhabi Islam—the puritanical Saudi variety favored by bin Laden —and the fastest growing variety of Islam in the Balkans. Today, in general, the Balkans are left without the money, political resources, or institutional strength to fight a war on terrorism. And that, for the Balkan Islamists, is a Godsend."*

Franken is right, with 20/20 hindsight, that Presidents Reagan and Bush Sr. made a bad mistake when they trained and armed bin Laden and his followers in Afghanistan to fight the Soviet invasion. Of course, bin Laden had not declared war on the United States back then. The Cold War was not over and we made a pact with bin Laden to fight a common enemy, for which we have paid a considerable price.

But Clinton had eight years to reverse course and prevent a brush fire from turning into a conflagration. He had multiple opportunities to end the al Qaeda threat **after bin Laden's declaration of war but before bin Laden could carry out his total plan**. Instead, except for a couple of feeble missile strikes, Clinton let the threat grow out of control. He repeated the Reagan-Bush mistake nearly twenty years later - this time in the Balkans.

Al Franken makes a big deal of the fact that Clinton signed a piece of paper authorizing bin Laden's assassination and that his Administration even handed George Bush a "comprehensive plan to take out al Qaeda" a whole month before George Bush's inauguration. Big freaking deal! After eight long years of doing nothing in the face of two declarations of war and multiple homicidal attacks on Americans, Clinton signs a meaningless piece of paper and issues a plan for action for his successor to carry out. How pathetic! Even Franken's alter-ego Stuart Smalley is blushing.

Myth #3 - There is nothing linking Saddam Hussein's Iraqi regime to Al Qaeda.

This is the ostrich argument - those who believe it have their heads in the sand. They are unable to connect a few simple dots tying together common motive, opportunity and means.

We have already talked about the common motives and mutual interests that made Hussein and al Qaeda such natural allies. They were a veritable mutual admiration society if their own words are to be believed. Bin Laden did not care how many Muslims Saddam had killed. In fact, bin Laden – the Sunni fanatic – was all too happy with Saddam's suppression and massacre of the hated infidel Shiites. And Saddam and bin Laden were joined together in a holy war against the United States. Why else would bin Laden spend time in his second fatwa against the United States making Saddam look like the victim rather than the aggressor against other Muslim states that he really was?

> *"...despite the great devastation inflicted on the Iraqi people by the crusader-Zionist alliance, and despite the huge number of those killed, which has exceeded 1 million...despite all this, the Americans are once against trying to repeat the horrific massacres, as though they are not content with the protracted blockade imposed after the ferocious war or the fragmentation and devastation. So here they come to annihilate what is left of this people and to humiliate their Muslim neighbors."* (Jihad Against Jews and Crusaders World Islamic Front Statement 23 February 1998)

And the Saddam regime was effusive in its praise of bin Laden. The newspaper Babil, owned by one of Saddam's deceased sons Odai, published a poem written in homage to bin Laden. "All America is trying to kill me and I wish to die while fighting," says one line. The poet portrays bin Laden as a lonely figure enduring "the oppression of the enemy" (*Source: Kurdistan Observer, Associated Press report by Waiel Faleh, October 14, 2001*).

This mutual admiration society did more than exchange poems. Here are just a few examples of key links between Saddam's regime and al Qaeda in furtherance of their unholy alliance - connecting the dots between motive, opportunity and means to carry out their common nefarious objective *(sources include the Daily Telegraph, Jane Foreign Reports and National Standard)*:

- Mohammed Atta, the ringleader of the September 11th highjack, was hosted by the terrorist Abu Nidal at his house in Iraq. Headed simply "Intelligence Items", and dated July 1, 2001, a memo to Saddam signed by Tahir Jalil Habbush al-Tikriti, the former head of the Iraqi Intelligence Service (IIS) states that Mohammed Atta came with Abu Ammer (an Arabic nom-de-guerre - his real identity is unknown) to Abu Nidal's house: "We arranged a work programme for him for three days with a team dedicated to working with him… He displayed extraordinary effort and showed a firm commitment to lead the team which will be responsible for attacking the targets that we have agreed to destroy."

- On February 19, 1998, about six months prior to the attacks in Africa, Iraqi intelligence officials set in motion a plan to bring a senior and trusted bin Laden aide to Baghdad from Khartoum. An Iraqi intelligence document shows that a recommendation was made for "…the deputy director general to bring the [bin Laden] envoy to Iraq because we may find in this envoy a way to maintain contacts with bin Laden." The meetings took place in March 1998.

- Iraq's former intelligence chief, Farouk Hijazi, met with bin Laden in Sudan in 1994 and in Afghanistan in December 1998. Bin Laden visited Bagdad in January 1998 and met with Iraq Deputy foreign Minister Tariq Aziz for the purpose of establishing al Qaeda training camps in Iraq.

- Mahmdouh Mahmud Salim, who was involved in the bombings of the U.S. embassies in Kenya and Tanzania, also served as al liaison between Saddam and bin Laden during the 1990's.

- After the Cole attack, two al Qaeda terrorists went to Iraq for training in weapons of mass destruction and to bring back information on poisonous gases.

- According to Israeli sources quoted by Jane's Foreign Report on September 19, 2001, during the prior two years Iraqi intelligence officers were "shuttling between Baghdad and Afghanistan, meeting with Ayman Al Zawahiri." According to the sources, one of the Iraqi intelligence officers was captured by the Pakistanis near the border with Afghanistan.

The question is not whether Iraqi complicity in September 11th can be demonstrated beyond a reasonable doubt. That's a red herring. When war has been declared on America by a global network of fanatic terrorists who have already carried out a brutal attack on this country, the Commander-in-Chief cannot wait for enough evidence to convince a jury before removing a dangerous state sanctuary in the most volatile region of the world. I think it is time for the ostriches to take their heads out of the sand, give up their fantasies and confront the real world.

Myth #4 - The French were acting with the best moral intentions as our good friends by trying to pursue a peaceful resolution of the Iraqi conflict and helping us avoid war at all cost.

The French are usually late to realize a gathering danger. After pretending that Hitler was not a threat, they built the useless Maginot Line as a defense against Hitler's advancing troops. Twenty years after Winston Churchill delivered his "Iron Curtain" speech and the United States launched its policy of containment against the spread of Communism, France continued to focus on the long dead threat of Fascism as the number one evil and did not really focus on the evils of Communism until its iron hand became so obvious during the 1968 suppression of the Czech revolt.

Today, France has a seething Muslim population - the largest in Europe. First generation Muslim youths born in France are unemployed and living in squalid conditions, alienated from French society and thus representing the perfect recruits for the Islamist fanatics who have always hated France's extremely secularist culture and never forgave France for Napolean's invasions of Arab lands. The French government added fuel to the fire with its recent edict against public display of religious symbols in its schools - making a separatist radical Islamic education a more attractive alternative to the alienated. This mix has all the ingredients of a time bomb ready to explode - the fanatics have a ready-made terrorist infrastructure pointing a dagger at France in the heart of Europe.

Did the feckless French seriously think that Saddam Hussein would have come to their rescue somehow against the terrorists or that their friendship with Saddam would have kept the terrorists away? If so, they were in a state of complete denial. And once again, the United States will turn out to be France's true friend if the time comes to protect their way of life against those bent on destroying it. Couldn't France for once give the United States the benefit of the doubt in how best to prevent such a calamity?

Not a chance. The French were looking solely after the French, just like they always have. We have already discussed Sheikh Iraq's corrupt bargain with Saddam to secure the oil rights for his patron, Total Fina Elf. Nor did France want to jeopardize repayment of their four billion dollars of loans to the ruthless dictator. France had no compunctions violating the U.N. Charter by doing billions of dollars of business with Saddam in the face of the Security Council's embargo and was angling for more.

According to a report in the April 28, 2003 edition of the British newspaper The Daily Telegraph, papers found in the Iraqi foreign ministry show how, as recently as three years ago, French diplomats from the Quai d'Orsay were colluding with agents from IRIS (the Iraqi Intelligence Service, better known as the Mukhabarat) to frustrate efforts by the Iraqi opposition and the British-based human rights group Indict to highlight atrocities in Iraq at a conference in Paris. Other documents include a warm thank-you letter from Saddam to Chirac in response to the French President's campaign to end U.N. sanctions, a deal between Peugeot and Baghdad, and mysterious payments from IRIS to beneficiaries in France.

The French were playing both sides right up to the end - offering an endless series of diplomatic "solutions" at the United Nations to avoid war, while whispering assurances in Saddam's ear that they would never let the United Nations actually enforce its own resolutions.

I know the French are tired of hearing that they owe us their support for liberating them twice in the twentieth century. After all, they argue, Americans owe the French our very existence for fighting by our side in the American Revolution. To the French I say "merci" for the French monarchy's help in the fight against its arch enemy, the English. But lest we forget, even back then France was playing both sides to make money - sound familiar? France violated a 1713 treaty with England and opened its ports to American privateers who attacked British merchant ships at will and stole their cargo. That served France's interest in weakening British commercial power. But it also served France's monetary interests because, as insurance premiums rose to astronomical levels for British merchant ships, the French were all too willing to take British goods onto French ships for a hefty fee:

> *"Premiums for insurance of British ships sky-rocketed, even if the ship was in a convoy. In England, merchants began losing money, and actually began hiring French ships to transport their goods. The French ships, were never attacked by the American privateers. France made money, the Americans terrorized the British at home, and the British began to wonder if these colonies were worth keep-*

ing." (Source: The Privateers and the American Revolution, published online by PageWise, Inc.)

Inspired by the model of the American Revolution, the French went ahead with their own revolution and overthrew their king and queen. But a funny thing happened on the way to Liberte, Egalite, and Fraternite. Heads literally rolled and blood spilled down the boulevards of Paris as the revolutionaries turned on each other and guillotined anyone not willing to conform completely to the strictures of the Republic of Virtue. The French Revolution became the model for the fanatical regimes of more recent times.

True to form, the French forgot about their moral principles of freedom when they were ready to side with the slave-owning Southern Confederacy against the Union during our Civil War. They didn't care what Abraham Lincoln was fighting for, even after the Emancipation Proclamation made it clear that freeing the slaves was a principal objective. France, under Napoleon III, tried to broker an armistice between the North and the South and held open the possibility of officially recognizing the Confederacy and intervening if the North did not go along. He tried a little multilaterism of his own by enlisting the aid of England and Russia but got nowhere. What Napoleon III really wanted was a weakened United States so that he could establish a beachhead in Mexico. It worked for a little while but in the end France backed down when Lincoln's Administration called France's bluff.

And even though the United States fought for France's liberty in two World Wars - and lost more troops fighting to liberate France in World War II than the French did themselves - France went out of its way to thumb its nose at the United States. It opposed the United States in liberating millions of Iraqis from the torture chambers of Saddam Hussein and protecting the world against the real possibility that Sadam's development of weapons of mass destruction could end up serving madmen like Osama bin Laden. Once again, the French put their prestige and short-term economic interests over any moral principle greater than themselves.

They didn't just voice their opposition to President Bush's policies as they had every right to do. They tried to bully the Eastern and Central European countries, who were just beginning to taste the fruits of freedom—threatening to block their entry into the European Union if they continued to speak their conscience in support of the United States' overthrow of a dictatorship as brutal as the ones they had so recently experienced themselves. After an emergency summit on Iraq on Feb. 17, 2003, Chirac rebuked future members of the European Union for siding with the United States, saying they "should have kept quiet."

So much for the French mantra of multilateral cooperation and consensus that they want to ram down the United States' throat when it suits them.

We will have more to say about the French in the next chapter.

Myth #5 - The Iraqi war violated the United Nations Charter. It was an illegal use of force because it was not approved by the Security Council, which has the "sole" authority to declare war against a sovereign nation.

This argument rests on three false premises.

The first false premise is that the Security Council has exclusive jurisdiction with regard to deciding whether military action can be taken against a sovereign state. Nowhere in the United Nations Charter does it say anything of the kind. The Council has "primary" responsibility to act on behalf of the member states to try to maintain international peace and security. But it has no more than the powers conferred on it by the member states as their common agent against a menace to such peace and security. The member states do not lose their own sovereign powers to act, particularly after they have given the Security Council ample opportunity to enforce its own decisions.

In fact, France itself violated Article 2 of the U.N. Charter by continuing to provide assistance to Iraq during the period of economic sanctions imposed by the Security Council. Principle 5 of the Charter says that all Member States "shall refrain from giving assistance to any state against which the United Nations is taking preventive or enforcement action".

In the period between 1996 and 1998, the French sabotaged the U.N. inspection process, pushing for immediately lifting sanctions and for a clean bill of health for Iraq even though the U.N. inspections were not finished. A report commissioned by the French parliament published in September, 2002 puts the value of French exports to Iraq since sanctions were imposed at $3.5 billion. France's Total Fina Elf was poised to win contracts to drill the largest unexploited oil reserves in the world. From 1981 to 2001, according to the Stockholm International Peace Research Institute (SIPRI), France was responsible for over 13 percent of Iraq's arms imports.

In short, France and its allies did everything they could to obstruct the processes of the Security Council right up to the end. Then they lament how George Bush purportedly violated international law by moving ahead against Saddam. It reminds me of the child who, after killing both of his parents, pleads for the court's mercy because he is now an orphan.

In any event, there is recent precedent for military action taken outside of the United Nations where there was no imminent threat to any of the participants. The decision to wage war on Milosevic never came before the United Nations and was arguably interference in a domestic problem concerning the former nation of Yugoslavia in violation of Article 2 (Principle 4) of the U.N. Charter, which says that "(A)ll Members shall refrain in their international relations from the threat or use of force against the territorial integrity or political independence of any state, or in any other manner inconsistent with the Purposes of the United Nations."

If the defenders of the war on Milosevic can justify such action solely on the basis of ending ethnic cleansing in Kosovo and Bosnia (all previously parts of Yugoslavia), certainly the undisputed genocide committed by Saddam against his own people and his neighbors is no less a compelling justification for action after twelve years of consultation within the U.N. And can the feckless French seriously claim that President Bush's final decision to resort to military force violated international law when France itself has intervened with impunity in the affairs of sovereign African nations without any Security Council consultation, much less authorization?

The second false premise is the assertion that the Security Council did not already provide the appropriate authority for the United States and its coalition partners to use force against Saddam Hussein. Seventeen resolutions over 12 years, that Saddam Hussein continually defied, provided ample authority. The Security Council's finding in Resolution 1441 that Saddam was in material breach under the ceasefire with Iraq that ended the first Gulf War provided ample authority. The United States, as an individual party to that ceasefire, also had its own authority to take whatever action it deemed necessary to enforce the cease fire. The truth is that with Saddam's continuous firing on U.S and British aircraft protecting the no-fly zones, Iraq never really ceased firing and the U.S had every right under international law to defend itself and remove the threat to peace posed by Saddam Hussein once and for all.

The third false premise is the assertion that President Bush did not take all appropriate measures short of war as prescribed in the U.N. Charter before making the decision to use military force against Saddam. All the peaceful measures that the Charter lays out - including economic boycott -were tried without success for twelve long years. Nevertheless, President Bush went back to the Security Council for a resolution giving Saddam a clear warning that he had one last chance to prove that he was in full and unconditional compliance with all the resolutions. Saddam was told that he had to give the U.N. inspectors unrestricted access and prove that he had destroyed all of his stockpiles of weapons of mass destruction. The burden was on him to prove his compliance, not on the U.S to catch him with a "smoking gun". Nobody, including even the feckless French, has suggested that Saddam came close to complying.

The United States did not have to go back to the Security Council yet again before it had the right to take action. When President Bush did go back anyway in order to get the Security Council on record to unambiguously enforce its own prior resolutions, Chirac ran interference for his buddy Saddam.

When a member state brings a dispute to the Security Council to resolve, it does so *"without prejudice to the rights, claims, or position of the parties concerned"* (Article 40). The Security Council is given certain responsibilities by the member states to act on their behalf for maintaining peace and security. The Security Council had already spoken sufficiently. It was time to take decisive action.

George Bush brought the United Nations back to its foundation for success, as articulated by Winston Churchill. Chirac may want to read what this great world leader had to say about his hopes for an effective United Nations after Churchill helped lead the free world to victory over Hitler:

> *A world organization has already been erected for the prime purpose of preventing war, UNO, the successor of the League of Nations, with the decisive addition of the United States and all that means, is already at work. We must make sure that its work is fruitful, that it is a reality and not a sham, that it is a force for action, and not merely a frothing of words, that it is a true temple of peace in which the shields of many nations can some day be hung up, and not merely a cockpit in a Tower of Babel. Before we cast away the solid assurances of national armaments for self-preservation we must be certain that our temple is built, not upon shifting sands or quagmires, but upon the rock* (Winston Churchill's Sinews of Peace Address, March 5, 1946 Westminster College, Fulton, Missouri).

Myth #6 - President Bush knew all along that there were no weapons of mass destruction (WMD) in Iraq. He deliberately lied to the American people to justify his aggressive war plans.

President Bush's detractors gleefully point to the recent statements by David Kay, the former U.S. arms inspector and head of the U.S.-led Iraq Survey Group, disclaiming the existence of any WMD in Iraq right before the war, as proof positive of Bush's "big WMD lie." They leap from after-the-fact discovery of a mistaken belief to suspicions of pre-war conspiratorial prevarication.

Senator John Kerry, the Democrats' presumed Presidential nominee, shares these suspicions and accuses President Bush of duplicity in his reliance on WMD as a justification for the war - even though Kerry had reached the same conclusions based on the same evidence. Revealingly, this is the same John Kerry who accused his own Government and his military superiors of "war crimes" and "criminal hypocrisy" in connection with the Vietnam War thirty years ago. While Kerry now brags about his heroism in Vietnam, here is what he had to say about his own conduct and the conduct of his superiors in 1971:

> *I committed the same kind of atrocities as thousands of other soldiers have committed in that I took part in shootings in free fire zones. I conducted harassment and interdiction fire. I used 50 calibre machine guns, which we were granted and ordered to use, which were our only weapon against people. I took part in search and destroy missions, in the burning of villages. All of this is contrary to the laws of warfare, all of this is contrary to the Geneva Conventions and all of this is ordered as a matter of written established policy by the government of the United States from the top down. And I believe that the men who designed these, the men who designed the free fire zone, the men who ordered us, the men who signed off the air raid strike areas, I think these men, by the letter of the law, the same letter of the law that tried Lieutenant Calley, are war criminals.* (Source: Audiotape, April 18, 1971 of John Kerry's "Meet the Press" interview"; see also Winter Soldier speech to Senate Foreign Relations Cmte Apr 23, 1971).

Flash forward to 2004. We find Kerry spewing forth the same kind of intemperate rehotoric at the President of the United Sates who is trying to protect the American people against another 9/11. Only this time Kerry is supposed to be a responsible candidate for the Presidency himself.

Then as now, Kerry and his liberal friends turn a reasonable debate over policy choices into a dark conspiracy of lies and deceit. But before anyone can rationally infer a lie from David Kay's findings on WMD, one must consider whether it was reasonable to assume that WMD had existed based on the imperfect information available and the consequences of making the wrong decision in such circumstances.

Consider that Kay himself admitted that he was wrong in originally expecting that WMD did exist, which he was only able to disprove after he scoured Iraq with the kind of thorough inspection that the U.N. inspectors could only dream of as long as Saddam remained in power (and lets not forget that the U.N. inspectors themselves had believed such weapons existed and complained that Saddam's regime had impeded their search). Kay did say, however, that "We've found a strong body of evidence with regard to the intentions of Saddam Hussein to continue to attempt to acquire WMD" (*Source: BBC interview, October 2003*). Kay also stated that "I think at the end of the inspection process, we'll paint a picture of an Iraq that was far more dangerous than even we thought it was before the war. It was of a system collapsing. It was a country that had the capability in weapons-of-mass-destruction areas and in which terrorists, like ants to honey, were going after it" (*Source: American Forces Press Service, January 29, 2004, reporting on statements made by David Kay when he appeared before the Senate Armed Services Committee on January 28, 2004*).

Consider that Senators (including John Kerry) and Representatives of both parties believed that WMD existed when they examined the same intelligence information that the Bush Administration relied upon in deciding to forcibly remove Saddam. In October 2002, Kerry asked in a Senate floor speech, "And while the administration has failed to provide any direct link between Iraq and the events of September 11th, can we afford to ignore the possibility that Saddam Hussein might...allow those weapons to slide off to one group or other in a region where weapons are the currency of trade?"

Consider that Prime Minister Tony Blair - at far greater political risk than Bush and with not even the appearance of any commercial incentives - committed British troops to the war because the evidence convinced him that Saddam's WMD program was "active, detailed and growing." The independent Hutton investigation exonerated Blair from charges that he purposefully exaggerated British intelligence assessments to justify his war policy.

Consider that Saddam had previously used chemical weapons and failed to account for stockpiles of chemical and biological agents found during earlier inspections. And consider Saddam's bizarre behavior right before the war. If he had nothing to hide, why didn't he open up his country entirely to unconditional U.N. inspections as South Africa has done and Libya is now doing?

Taking Kay's report at face value, President Bush no doubt relied on defective intelligence information, meriting an independent investigation of the quality of the intelligence gathering operations. But Bush certainly had strong reasons to believe the information presented to him at the time - especially in the context of more than 12 years of Saddam's warlike behavior. And Saddam had the last clear chance to come clean and avoid war, but chose not to do so. He paid the ultimate price for his own arrogance.

The bottom line is that whether or not motivated by mistaken intelligence about weapons of mass destruction, Bush's decision to take action brought about the destruction of a brutal and malignant dictatorship. With imperfect information and an impotent world body paralyzed by France's intransigence, Bush had to choose between the lesser of two evils - either do nothing, let Saddam continue to play hide-and-seek with the U.N. inspectors and hope for the best (with potentially disastrous consequences if the worst fears proved true) or force the end of a brutal, aggressive regime once and for all even if the worst fears proved unfounded. Call it President Bush's Wager against a Malignant Dictatorship (a different sort of "WMD", if you will). Bush forced Saddam's hand. Saddam thought he could bluff his way out of trouble with his usual lies and defiance, but this time he lost the wager. The Iraqi people were the winners while other malignant megalomaniacs - Osama bin Laden included - took notice, changing their tune from contempt of U.S. weakness to concern over U.S. resolve.

Whatever the foolish and feckless want to believe, President Bush's decision to wage war against this malignant dictatorship was a rational wager to end the uncertainty over the threat of weapons of mass destruction that Saddam himself deliberately perpetrated. As David Kay himself concluded:

"I will just say I'm convinced myself, if I had been there, presented (with) what I have seen as the record of the intelligence estimates, I probably would have come to - not probably - I would have come to the same conclusion that the political leaders did" and that the decision to go to war was "absolutely prudent."

One can still make a rational argument that faulty intelligence and hasty judgment led to a mistaken policy in Iraq and can debate these points in the political arena. Reasonable people can differ on how best to assess and act upon the imperfect evidence that was available at the time. But history will be the judge of the correctness of the policy, as it always is. And history looks more at consequences with the perspective of time, than worry about every reason articulated and passion at work when the decision was made.

The foolish liberals are too impatient for this. They want to create a false record now of what has happened in Iraq and the motivations for the war, hoping that it will later become the official history. Forgetting all the other valid reasons President Bush and his Administration have cited for the war all along, including Iraq's violation of multiple UN resolutions, the continuing killing fields of Saddam's regime, and hopes to create a flourishing democracy for the Iraqi people, the liberals focus exclusively on Iraq's WMD program or lack thereof.

The centerpiece of revisionism is their misquoting of President Bush's January, 2003 State of the Union Address - particularly those famous sixteen words dealing with Saddam's efforts to obtain enriched uranium from Africa. Al Franken, the Democrats' favorite clown, is apparently referring to that speech when he says that "the much-hyped uranium from Niger" was all part of a "disinformation campaign" that "emanated from the highest reaches of the government." These are strong words coming from the self-appointed guardian of the truth except they conveniently overlook what the President actually said in that one controversial sentence, not to mention ignoring completely the uncontroverted evidence concerning Saddam's biological and chemical programs - *"The British government has learned that Saddam Hussein recently sought significant quantities of uranium from Africa".*

Note that the British still stand by the accuracy of their information that Saddam **sought** uranium from Africa, but the liberals don't bother to mention that fact. Maybe the CIA didn't believe one of the sources for this information - a discredited document that was believed to have been forged - but the

British claim they had other credible sources. And as we all know, the CIA is not the end all and be all of intelligence.

Interestingly enough, one of the British sources may have been the French intelligence services who would not allow the U.K. to reveal this source- yes our friends the feckless French again doing their best to play both ends against the middle.

The July 10, 2003 edition of the London Daily Telegraph reports as follows:

> *The French secret service is believed to have refused to allow Britain's MI6 to give the United States "credible" intelligence showing that Iraq was trying to buy uranium ore from Niger, U.S. intelligence sources said yesterday. Britain's Secret Intelligence Service had more than one "different and credible" piece of intelligence to show that Iraq was attempting to buy the ore, known as yellowcake, British officials insisted. But it was given to them by at least one and possibly two intelligence services and, under the rules governing cooperation, it could not be shared with anyone else without the originator's permission. U.S. intelligence sources believe the most likely source of the MI6 intelligence was the French secret service, the DGSE. Niger is a former French colony, and its uranium mines are run by a French company that comes under the control of the French Atomic Energy Commission.*

Were the French concerned that some back channel dealing to help Saddam, involving Sheikh Iraq's pals in French business and their connections with Niger, would come to light? Perhaps. But one thing is clear - the only disinformation concerning the Niger uranium claim came out of Franken and his liberal friends' mouths. They misrepresented what President Bush actually said in his State of the Union Address and forgot to mention that the British still stood by their sources.

It is bad enough when the foolish liberals try to re-write what President Bush actually said. But since Al Gore has become their poster-boy, we find an outbreak of amnesia on what the Vice President had to say about weapons of mass destruction when he was in a position of responsibility.

Al Gore is now a favorite of the ultra-liberal Move-On organization, the group that was formed to persuade the country to "move on" from dealing with former President Clinton's real perjury under oath and is now dedicated to bringing down President Bush for daring to tell the world the truth about Saddam Hussein.

Apparently Al Gore is like the Gollum character in the Lord of the Rings, whose brain is divided into a good side and bad side. Al's left brain (his "good" side in the eyes of his new-found liberal friends) has forgotten what his right brain (his "bad" side as far as the liberals are concerned, known in French as "Mal") had said about Saddam when Gore was Vice President. For example, in 1998 Mal Gore supported the Iraq Liberation Act, calling for the removal of Hussein. And as a candidate for president in 2000, Mal said, *"We have made it clear that it is our policy to see Saddam Hussein gone."* Mal Gore even displayed some backbone when he asserted: *"And if entrusted with the presidency, my resolve will never waver."*

Mal Gore agreed with President Bush as recently as September, 2002 about the weapons of mass destruction:

> *"We know that he has stored secret supplies of biological and chemical weapons throughout his country."* Al Gore, Sept. 23, 2002

> *"Iraq's search for weapons of mass destruction has proven impossible to deter and we should assume that it will continue for as long as Saddam is in power."* Al Gore, Sept. 23, 2002

But less than a year later, in a speech sponsored by Move-On, Al's left brain took over. The war against Iraq was all wrong. It had nothing to do with the war against terrorism. Bush should have ignored the report from British intelligence concerning Saddam's attempts to get enriched uranium from Africa - even though the British still stand by it today. Saddam really didn't have to go after all. It was no longer worth doing what was necessary to see "Saddam Hussein gone."

Of course, Al Gore forgot Mal Gore's earlier warnings about Saddam. He also forgot his boss's warning that ... *"Saddam Hussein must not be allowed to threaten his neighbors or the world with nuclear arms, poison gas or biological weapons... left unchecked, Saddam Hussein will use these terrible weapons again."*

Not a word in Al Gore's Move-On speech about Saddam's biological or chemical weapons programs. Total silence on Saddam's search for "weapons of mass destruction" that has "proven impossible to deter". Even to a liberal audience that should applaud the liberation of 25 million people from horrible human rights abuses, Al Gore preferred to excoriate Bush as public enemy #1 over tax cuts for the wealthy and supposed infractions of civil liberties.

If Al Gore and his liberal friends are correct today in condemning Bush more than they condemn Saddam, one can only surmise that President Clinton and Mal Gore did not mean what they said back in 1998 when they warned the country about Saddam and Clinton said that "Iraq has abused its final chance". How many final chances is this dictator supposed to get? Or perhaps they truly believe, against all evidence, that Saddam decided to reform his ways after all, but that the hawks in the Bush Administration were hell-bent on war anyway.

I think there is a much simpler answer. Liberals are not willing to use raw military power and take risks to defend American interests, even where strategic and moral imperatives converge. Evil is a relative term to them. They think that even the worst offender can be brought around eventually through reasoned discussion under international law. Since the United States has its own unworthy motives in their eyes - oil, for example - we have no greater moral standing than any other nation in the world to impose our will. Unable to distinguish between right and wrong and overlooking the tide of history toward democracy led by the United States as it vanquished Nazi and Communist totalitarianism in turn, the liberals prefer to stand with what Ambassador Jeane Kirpatrick called the Blame America First crowd. Perhaps in their mind unless one is perfect - an impossible state to achieve for human beings - we are all no better than anybody else. This is a pessimistic view of human potential that is at odds with the American experience.

Myth #7 - The Iraqi war was illegitimate because it was all about oil.

This is another favorite liberal myth. It reminds me of the old Groucho Marx TV show "You Bet Your Life" where the duck came down only if you said the "magic word". In the liberals' way of thinking, since President Bush did not justify the war from the very beginning with the magic words "human rights", it does not matter that the war led directly to the toppling of a brutal regime responsible for the death of hundreds of thousands of innocent people.

Suppose for the moment that the primary motive was oil, not a lofty moral cause like human rights. The immediate dividend is still the end to a brutal regime. Do the foolish liberals believe that Iraq is worse off today with Saddam pulled out of his spider hole and now in prison? Perhaps they should consider the findings of the Human Rights Watch World Report 2003, based on conditions before the Saddam regime was toppled:

> *The Iraqi government continued to commit widespread and gross human rights violations, including the extensive use of the death penalty and the extrajudicial execution of prisoners, the forced expulsion of ethnic minorities from government-controlled areas in the oil-rich region of Kirkuk and elsewhere, the arbitrary arrest of suspected political opponents and members of their families, and the torture and ill-treatment of detainees…Government opponents and relatives of political detainees continued to report numerous executions of political suspects and those convicted of ordinary criminal offenses, as well as former army personnel suspected of disloyalty to the authorities… The government continued to implement its "Arabization" policy of forcibly expelling Kurdish, Turkman, and Assyrian families from their homes in areas under its control in Kirkuk, Khaniqin, Sinjar, and other areas, and replacing them with Arab families brought from southern Iraq. The vast majority of those expelled were Kurds, who were moved to Kurdish-held areas in the northern provinces, with a smaller number expelled to southern Iraq. In September, Human Rights Watch interviewed scores of expelled Kurdish and Turkman families, some within days of their expulsion. Officials forced them to leave their homes with very few*

personal possessions, and stripped them of all documentation except for their identity cards. In the majority of cases, one immediate reason for expulsion was their refusal to sign the so-called nationality correction forms, which were introduced by the government in 1997 to force non-Arabs to alter their ethnic identity by registering as Arabs. Other reasons included their refusal to join the Ba'th Party or the failure of male family members to undergo military training for the Jerusalem Army (Jaysh al-Quds) or, in the case of children age twelve through seventeen, for Saddam's Cubs (Ashbal Saddam). Many reported that the government continued to ban the use of non-Arab names when registering newborns, and that in some cases they pressured non-Arabs to adopt Arab names upon marriage.

This was just the tip of the iceberg, as the discovery of mass graves by coalition forces attests. The film clips of executions that were taken from the archives of the General Security directorate, Saddam Hussein's most powerful secret police agency, display the horrors all too clearly for those willing to open their eyes to see. Maybe the foolish liberals would lose a little of their smugness if they spoke to an Iraqi like Dr. Taki al-Moosawi who got the chance recently to view a film clip of his nephew, whom he had not seen since 1984, being blown apart by a grenade that one of Chemical Ali's lackeys had taped to the nephew's chest. Maybe the liberals should even see the film themselves, especially the part when the execution party walks away laughing and congratulating each other for one more unfathomable murder, led by Chemical Ali who went on to even greater glory in the service of his master when he commanded troops into Kuwait in 1990. Perhaps they will then feel just a wee bit of pride that Chemical Ali is now a guest of Uncle Sam, captured by American troops in August 2003 (*Source: New York Times, December 31, 2003*).

But what if the liberals are conceivably right in their suspicions about original motivations, and they can prove somehow that the war was started because of oil? I don't believe it for a moment since we could have obtained oil alot more easily by simply seizing the oil fields of Saudi Arabia and Kuwait where we already had our troops stationed. But I also don't care. I have no problem with American companies doing well while their government accomplished something so profoundly good for a long-suffering people.

Lets take a closer look at the so-called oil motive on its own terms, pretending for the moment as the liberals do that the benefit achieved for human rights should not be considered if the original motive for going into Iraq with military force was impure in the eyes of the self-appointed arbiters of what constitutes a "just war".

Securing the world's major oil fields to avoid potential economic catastrophe is not a bad thing. History shows that the major oil companies make more money, while users in developed and undeveloped countries suffer, from spikes in oil prices that result from disruptions to the world's oil supply. Stabilizing the oil supply means stable oil prices. Keeping oil bottlenecks out of the hands of terrorists means stable oil prices.

Saudi Arabia is at best a fair weather friend, which has been both the breeding ground for terrorism and is now its prime target. We cannot depend on Saudi Arabia as our critical source of supply of Arab oil. The militant fundamentalist ideology that is the source of Islamic fanaticism is centered in Saudi Arabia. The royal family has tried to tame the beast to no avail. Some members would even like to see it succeed because they believe in the rhetoric.

And bin Laden has made no secret of his ambition to return to his homeland as conqueror over all "infidel" interests. With help from sympathizers in Saudi Arabia, terrorists could simultaneously hit several sensitive points in the oil infrastructure from eight of Saudi Arabia's largest oil fields. This action alone could knock the Saudis out of the oil business for about two years, create economic havoc in Saudi Arabia and in the West, and make bin Laden's takeover a cakewalk.

A stable and economically successful Iraq buffers us against chaos in Saudi Arabia, not to mention that it provides us our best platform for preventing a terrorist take-over there. Instead of using shaky Saudi Arabia as a base to fight Saddam's Iraq and fire up the fanatic Islamists in the process because our troops are on their holy land, we use a friendly and secure Iraq as a hedge against dangerous trends in Saudi Arabia, the fanatic Islamists' number one target.

These are worthy objectives in themselves, which will enhance the world's economic health and social well-being. Transferring Iraq's oil reserves (the second largest in the world) from hostile to friendly hands will accomplish this objective, while directing the revenues from Saddam's armaments and palaces to schools, infrastructure improvements and medical care for the Iraqi people. This isn't a pie-in-the-sky dream. It is happening right now, which is why the terrorists are doing everything they can to disrupt an orderly transition.

In short, establishing a stable, free and friendly country in the volatile Middle East with access to a major source of Arab oil is a critical part of the long-term war against terrorism.

Oil is bad enough a motive for the foolish liberals, but they really go crazy whenever the subject of Halliburton comes up. As The New York Times put it, Halliburton's Iraq contract "undermines the Bush administration's portrayal of the war as a campaign for disarmament and democracy, not lucre."

The liberals are correct in calling for a full investigation of Halliburton's questionable billing practices. If allegations of Halliburton's overcharges prove to be correct, civil penalties, and possibly criminal sanctions, are in order.

However, this is a far cry from concluding that the Bush Administration went to war because of Halliburton or that Halliburton was chosen as a boon to Vice President Cheney. Where is the evidence to support such bogus charges?

We do know that a number of prominent Frenchmen who supported Saddam Hussein's regime have been identified as recipients of oil contracts as part of Saddam Hussein's end run around the United Nations oil-for-food humanitarian program. This list, discovered in the files of the Iraqi Oil Ministry in Baghdad, included Patrick Maugein, a close political associate and financial backer of French President Jacques Chirac; Charles Pasqua, former minister of interior; and Bernard Merimee, former French ambassador to the United Nations (*Source: ABCNEWS.com, January 29, 2004*). So there is plenty of evidence of a French-Iraqi oil connection that was set up to keep Saddam in power. But the liberals ignore this real oil conspiracy and make up one about Halliburton.

The foolish liberals present no evidence that Halliburton was incompetent. After all, Halliburton performed well for Clinton in the Balkans. Vice President Gore's National Performance Review mentioned Halliburton's performance favorably in its Report on Reinventing the Department of Defense, issued in September 1996. Indeed, the Clinton Administration awarded a no-bid contract to Halliburton to continue its work in the Balkans supporting the U.S. peacekeeping mission there because it made little sense to change midstream. The Army's sole-source Bosnia contract with Halliburton's subsidiary Kellogg Brown & Root lasted until 1999. At that time, the Clinton Defense Department conducted full-scale competitive bidding for a new contract and chose Kellogg Brown & Root. The company continued its work in Bosnia uninterrupted.

The liberals present no evidence of wrong-doing in the selection process. The U.S. Army Logistics Civil Augmentation Program, known as LOGCAP, is a competitively bid multiyear contract for a corporation to be on call to provide whatever services might be needed quickly. Halliburton won the competitive bidding process for LOGCAP in 2001. Was it really dishonest or unethical to turn to Halliburton's wholly owned subsidiary Kellogg Brown & Root for prewar planning about handling oil fires in Iraq and rely on them afterward to implement their plans, all subject to continuing government audit and inspection? Any infractions that have been discovered are being addressed.

The liberals likewise present no evidence of profiteering by Halliburton. In fact, despite its editorial sloganeering, the New York Times news department has specifically reported after an extensive investigation that there was "no evidence of profiteering" by Halliburton. Indeed, there has been very little evidence of any profit at all - "minimal" in the words of the New York Times (*Source: New York Times, December 29, 2003*). Total company revenue and operating income from Iraq-related work in the third quarter of 2003 were $900 million and $34 million, respectively—about a 4% return. This beats inflation, but not much else.

And the liberals do not even have the decency of acknowledging that Halliburton has suffered its own fatalities. Since the war began in Iraq, at least three Halliburton employees have been killed - the results of a vehicle accident, an anti-tank mine, and a gunshot wound.

All the liberals can do is make the McCarthy-type charges based on guilt by association - Vice President Cheney used to be Halliburton's CEO so he must have pushed for his former company to reap the spoils of war. All I can say to that charge is that if the foolish liberals had put even a quarter of their time and brainpower into examining the evidence of dangerous links between al Qaeda and Saddam Hussein in the first place, maybe they really wouldn't care if an American company - rather than the French companies that Saddam enjoyed dealing with - is actually making a little bit of profit from the reconstruction effort.

Myth #8 - Concentration on Iraq has undermined the "war on terror".

This is the "cannot walk and chew gum at the same time" theory. The truth is that the war on terror has many fronts, including Iraq, and that we can and must strike the multi-tentacle enemy in different places and in different ways all at the same time. Since September 11th, the United States and its allies have fought two ground wars, captured or killed many key al Qaedi operatives, frozen their assets all over the world and thwarted multiple and widely dispersed terrorist plots.

The mythologists insist, however, that if we only devoted all our soldiers now in Iraq to the business of finding the ringleader Osama bin Laden, the war on terrorism could be won.

Too bad real life is not that simple.

First of all, does anyone seriously think that adding 150,000 troops to scour the thousands of miles of mountainous region between Afghanistan and Pakistan, where tribes loyal to Osama are in charge, stands more than an infinitesimal chance of success - even if it were logistically feasible and Osama were actually there? Our best chance is to continue relying on the right intelligence folks on the ground in Pakistan, who have already turned over several leading al Quadi operatives.

And even if we found him, does anyone seriously believe that the global terrorist network will suddenly disappear? Finding Osama and hastening his journey to his eternal paradise will constitute a great tactical victory for us and put a serious dent into the terrorists' ambitions, at least for the short term. It will be a great morale booster for us and a morale deflator for the bad guys. But the problem is that there are many Islamic fanatics as bad or worse than bin Laden. They are organized into a loose network of cells that produces new cells as old ones die, so long as the right conditions are there to feed upon. Osama's capture or demise will be a great accomplishment, but not nearly enough to kill the cancer of Islamic terrorism altogether, any more than radiation administered to a cancer patient that kills one cancer cell will automatically eradicate all the cancer cells in the body.

By all means, lets continue to go after bin Laden and cut al Qaeda down to size. But lets also realize that we need to fight the war strategically.

The key is to change the fundamental dynamics that nourish the terrorist malignancy.

First, I'll tell the foolish liberals what this doesn't mean. I am not referring to trying to understand the impoverished conditions of undeveloped countries that liberals love to cite as a leading cause of terrorism. The United States was the world's largest contributor of aid to Afghanistan while it was under Taliban rule, and we saw the results - a base for bin Laden's global network. I don't want to "feel their pain". I want to inflict maximum pain on the terrorists and their supporters.

I'm also not referring to more vigorous criminal prosecution of the terrorists, as if we were dealing with a Mafia don who we can take out by getting a Sammy the Bull type to turn states' evidence. Franken rhapsodizes how "the handsome, brilliant young President Clinton" swung into action after the 1993 bombing of the World Trade Center by capturing, trying, convicting, and imprisoning those responsible. Really? So since "Ramzi Yousef, Abdul Hakim Murad, and Wali Khan Amin Shah are all currently behind bars", how come they didn't turn states' evidence and tip us off about leads that could have prevented the terrorist strikes against our embassies in Kenya and Tanzania and the terrorist attack on the USS Cole, let alone the planning for September 11th that started in earnest during the Clinton years? Due process has no applicability to non U.S. citizens bent on destroying the very freedoms that make due process possible.

Heaven help us if we were to return to the days when the war on terror was regarded as "primarily" a "law enforcement operation" and only "occasionally military" as Senator Kerry seems to prefer (see Senator Kerry's remarks from the January 29, 2004 South Carolina Democratic Primary Debate). This thinking represents a colossal misunderstanding of the symbiotic global alliance of stateless fanatics and rogue state despots who use the vulnerabilities created by our freedoms to attack our defenses. These enemies will not be satisfied unless they can prove their invulnerability to their admirers by bringing the hated United States down. To do this, they have to escalate the realm of violence on multiple fronts to demonstrate our weakness before their twisted version of their "God". Against a well-funded global network of psychotics who can get their hands on horrific weapons to carry out their apocalyptic purposes, our traditional notions of law enforcement are useless.

We would merely be shooting blanks while the enemy will continue to shoot at us like fish in a barrel.

There is no question that effective law enforcement is a key tool we need for our homeland defense. But to stop this enemy we need most of all a forceful and relentless military strategy, backed by sound intelligence on the ground that is unconstrained by anachronistic legalisms. We need to bring the battle to the enemy - everywhere they hide and they get support. We must humiliate the terrorists and their sponsors with force to the point that their pretense to power is exposed to the world as devoid of all reality and their tattered remnants return to their spider holes and caves for good.

A strategically fought war creates surprise for the enemy with as many potential points of attack against them and their sponsors as the terrorists can launch against us. It keeps them off balance by bringing the fighting to their home court and it applies massive force as a deterrent - not against would-be martyrs who will die for their cause but against all of the sources that can aid and abet them. This is where Iraq comes in. A hostile Iraq is another source of nutrients that the terrorist cells need to survive - money, safe houses, arms, connections with other terrorists, bases for attacking Saudi Arabia, etc. A friendly Iraq dries up this swamp.

And then a reverse domino effect begins to take hold, as we already are seeing in Libya's sudden decision to discontinue its own weapons program and throw open its facilities to unlimited inspections. Together with the valuable intelligence that we have seized in Iraq as a result of the war, Libya will now take us inside the interlocking network of clandestine exchanges of nuclear technology, parts, sources of enriched uranium, money, and missile delivery systems that connect Pakistan, North Korea, Iran, Libya, and possibly Saudi Arabia in a symbiotic relationship that the terrorists are primed to exploit. Now the terrorists and their state sponsors have to figure out what we will learn and where we may go next to further unravel their network. Is it a coincidence that following Iraq, we are seeing Libya's reversal of course, Pakistan's withdrawal of support for Islamic militants in Kashmir and rapproachment with India, the beginnings of reforms in Saudi Arabia and even North Korea's agreement to allow an unofficial United States delegation to visit one of its nuclear weapons complexes? Perhaps, but highly unlikely. Left on their own, international inspectors have turned up nothing for years.

A thought provoking article by Fredric Smoler (who teaches literature, classics, and modern history at Sarah Lawrence College), published in the November/December 2001 edition of the American Heritage, provides some insights as to how to fight a strategic war on terrorism based on lessons learned from the past. In the article, entitled "Fighting the Last War - and the Next", the author questions whether a state's national sovereignty deserves any respect if it is used to cloak genocide at home and support for terrorism abroad in violation of the most minimal norms of civilized behavior. He asks the rhetorical question: "If we discover that a state has backed grievous assaults on us, should we in fact suspend the sovereignty of that state by force of arms - invasion, conquest, and the formation of a new regime?"

International law governing the right of national sovereignty under the protection of the United Nations - all inventions of the West to ensure peaceful co-existence - are turned against us by fanatics whose catastrophic goals are limited only by the means of destruction they possess. An unconventional war by psychotics with access to weapons of mass destruction demands the unconventional exercise of power by the only nation in the world capable of enforcing rules of civilized behavior.

If Iraq turns into a flowering democracy that sets off a chain reaction throughout the Muslim world, so much the better. Turning around Woodrow Wilson's famous promise to "make the world safe for democracy", we would be making the world democratic for the sake of genuine peace and security. Japan and Germany have not bothered any of their neighbors for nearly sixty years. There is certainly no inherent incompatibility between Islam and democracy. Turkey demonstrates that democracy can work in a Muslim country. Afghanistan has adopted a constitutional form of government that recognizes the rights of the minority.

But Iraq's history and splintered ethnic and religious groups make it especially tough soil to grow a successful democracy. And we have already suffered more casualties during the transition to self-rule than during the war itself. So why bother?

The answer is that democracy is a desirable but not a necessary outcome to justify the forcible ending of Saddam Hussein's genocidal, terrorist-sponsoring regime. In Iraq, the spirits of Mother Theresa and Machiavelli join hands because we did good by being smart.

For Mother Theresa, human rights has triumphed (*"Human rights are not a privilege conferred by government. They are every human being's entitlement by virtue of his humanity"*).

For Machiavelli, pragmatic strategy has triumphed (*"For ((taking into account all those things of which one can take advantage better than the many, which may be infinite)) this will always occur, that by using a little industry he will be able to disunite the many and make weak that body which was strong"*).

From a strategic point of view, we have scrambled the terrorists' calculations of our next moves and what we now know about them. We have sown disunity in the ranks of their supporters who no longer are so convinced that we will crumble under pressure. Bin Laden counted on a tough but proportionate response to September 11th and ended up hiding in a cave somewhere, losing the advantage of his state-sponsored sanctuary. Saddam spat in the world's face, expecting more tough words and a few bombs that he was willing to let his people absorb while building his stockpiles of dangerous arms, and ended up a totally humiliated shell of himself as he crawled out of his spider hole before the entire world. Treasure troves of valuable intelligence are now in our hands.

Far from undermining the war on terrorism, our decisive use of force in Iraq is part and parcel of the broader strategy to stay ahead of the enemy and keep them guessing as to where we will go next and how we will do it. In the past, we have acted defensively and in calculated, predictable steps within a set of rules that signal exactly what we were liable to do next - apply economic sanctions, prosecute the terrorists we manage to capture, fire a few missiles and wait for an attack before taking any forceful action and then only in proportion to the scope of the attack. Iraq changes the equation precisely because it was so out of character for how United States has handled terrorism prior to 9/11. Now we are in a better position to capitalize on the terrorists and their sponsors' lack of information of what our next move will be, just as they have capitalized on their use of surprise. After losing their own state sanctuary in Afghanistan and finding Pakistan a more unreliable source of weapons since President Musharraf's pivot toward the United States, the fanatic Islamists have striven to topple Musharraf and take over Pakistan. But our decisive action in Iraq forces the terrorists to re-calculate how the United States would react to such an occurrence. They can no longer discount the probability that after successes in Afghanistan and Iraq, we will do whatever it takes in Pakistan to secure their nuclear facilities (and in Saudi Arabia to secure their oil facilities) and keep them out of the fanatics' hands. And we can now use the platform we have in Iraq to more effectively combat the virulent Whabi religious fundamentalists of Saudi Arabia who provide recruits and funding for al Qaeda.

In the words of Michael Scott Doran, an assistant professor of Near Eastern Studies at Princeton in his essay appearing in Foreign Affairs magazine, entitled "The Dual Monarchy", *"Al Qaeda's nightmare scenario is that the Americans and the Iraqi Shiites will force Riyadh to enact broad reforms and bring the Saudi Shiites into the political community. There is no question that many hard-line Saudi clerics share precisely the same fears..."*

In game theory terms, the mortal damage we inflicted on Saddam's regime (including his sons' death and his own humiliating capture) has a multiplier effect by giving us a credible threat power advantage. Iraq is a clear demonstration of U.S. power and resolve. This is why Libya has reversed course and allowed unlimited inspections, with all the dividends that will ensue in exposing more parts of the interlocking network - dominos beginning to fall in a row. No country can act with impunity any longer - whether it is the usual suspects in Iran, North Korea or Syria or the terrorist sympathizers in Pakistan and Saudi Arabia.

We change behavior by making the next dictator of a rogue state nervous that he too will turn into the poor sap escorted out of a hole by our GIs. No doubt bin Laden will not be deterred as long as he keeps finding gullible followers to sacrifice for his cause. But the state sponsors he needs are motivated most of all by self-preservation. Saddam's fate was crucial in convincing other would-be sponsors that we won't be hemmed in by the niceties of international law, world opinion or domestic politics to do whatever we have to by whatever means to get rid of them. We are cutting off the nutrients necessary to the growth of the cancer cells one by one, unraveling the interlocking network with increased intelligence we gain from each of our attacks and draining their sources of funding.

Myth #9 - The Bush Administration is assaulting our civil liberties in the name of terrorism prevention.

This is the "Chicken Little, the sky is falling" argument that liberals love to make. We have lost our precious liberties. The constitution is being ripped to shreds.

Al Gore invokes George Orwell's 1984 and calls the Patriot Act "a broad and extreme invasion of our privacy rights in the name of terrorism prevention". How about the Internet that he invented? Isn't Gore a little nervous that Big Brother can track our every click stroke to put together a whole profile on us? And did he worry about civil liberties back in 1996 when the Clinton-Gore Administration passed the Antiterrorism Act in 1996 that contained many of the building blocks of the Patriot Act?

As a good student of history, Al Gore certainly knows that civil liberties have suffered far more during earlier crises this country has faced and that they have always come back stronger than ever. Abraham Lincoln suspended habeas corpus and locked up state legislators temporarily during the Civil War and we survived. Somehow this seems more serious than whether the government can find out what book I last took out of the library or bought from a book store. By the way, since the government hasn't come around to my apartment to conduct a search, it was Al Franken's Lies and the Lying Liars who Tell Them. And it struck me as I was reading Franken's non-stop tirade, inveighing against Bush, Cheny, Ashcroft and everyone else associated with this Administration as dirty liars—how was Franken able to get the book published and released in the kind of police state we are supposedly living in?

The Patriot Act does not eliminate the role of judges in questioning FBI agents before granting warrants. Covert wiretaps and a secret court to oversee domestic spy probes have been on the books since 1968 and 1978 respectively. Despite their doomsday forecasts of an emerging police state, the opponents of the Patriot Act have failed to present any credible evidence that the so-called "libraries" provision - allowing the FBI to obtain secret court orders in order to collect records it needs in terrorism or intelligence investigations - has even been used against any American citizen as they allege, let alone abused.

Nevertheless, Senator Kerry makes even more of a fool of himself than Al Gore by comparing the use of the Patriot Act that he voted for to the repression of Afghans by the Taliban (*Source: New York Times, March 6, 2004*). Does the Senator really think that investigating a terrorist suspect's reading habits is the moral equivalent of the Taliban's murder of thousands of Shiite Muslims in Afghanistan simply because the Taliban disagreed with the Shiites' practice of Islam? Or that increased surveillance of suspected financial transactions is comparable to the Taliban's repressive enforcement of their religious code, including the beatings and stoning of women to death who dared to display any desire for independence? In uttering such nonsense, Senator Kerry and other like-minded scaremongers have shown how terribly irresponsible they can be.

As if this were not enough, liberals have forgotten the horrible reality of September 11th. Returning to their extreme civil libertarian stance, they conveniently forget that all of the perpetrators of the September 11th attacks were of Middle Eastern origin. These Arab fanatics, mostly from Saudi Arabia, took advantage of the liberties afforded by our free society to enter our country and murder our people.

And what is Senator Kerry's response? He worries about how Arab visitors will feel when they are subjected to more careful screening and tracking. Apparently, their sensibilities are more important to him than the security of the American people.

Kerry is actually "outraged that the Justice Department has required tens of thousands of Muslim and Arab visa holders - students, workers, researchers, and tourists - to register with the government and be fingerprinted and photographed" (*Source: Letter to MoveOn.org members, June 17, 2003*).

Given the fact that the September 11th highjackers were all of Middle Eastern descent - some with visas - and that other would-be terrorists caught in this country and in Europe are also of Middle Eastern descent, is it so unreasonable to focus on these groups in enforcing our immigration laws? Why shouldn't we be able to better identify and track visitors from volatile areas and to immediately deport a suspicious alien who has no credible explanation for over-extending his visa or does not have proper credentials? Particularly when we understand that Islamic militants living in non-Muslim countries are told to harbor enmity and hatred for the infidels and that a key part of their strategy (Jehad) is to undermine their host countries from within and to recruit the disaffected for their causes - in the prisons and in their mosques, for example.

But look at all those poor fanatic Islamists being held indefinitely against their will in Guantanamo Bay without the right to even see a lawyer. Liberals cry crocodile tears over this. Such a shocking infringement of Constitutional liberties that the guardian of our liberties, the great Federal Ninth Circuit in California, had to intervene - you know, that particular Court of Appeals that so often finds itself being reversed.

Whose liberties, may I ask? I am willing to concede that a U.S. citizen captured on U.S soil, whatever the charge, is entitled to the Constitutional benefits of due process. Even Jose Padilla (a.k.a. Abdullah Al Muhajir), who has been accused of plotting to set off a "dirty bomb" and using the benefits of his U.S. citizenship to conspire with members of al Qaeda by scouting for them.

But since when do we turn our Constitution into an instrument of our own destruction by granting non-U.S. citizens, captured abroad in the course of participating in the fanatics' fight-to-the-death jihaad against us, anything but a cold cell and enough food to survive until we get all the intelligence we can possibly get out of them and then figure out in our own time what we should do with them? Out of the goodness of our hearts, we have given the fanatics an opportunity to pray to Allah. Do you suppose they are praying for forgiveness or are they apologizing to bin Laden for not dying in his cause, cursing the Great Satan or passing coded messages to each other? Does it really matter? They are out of harm's way. They chose their fate and can wallow in self-pity for the duration of their days on this Earth, for all I care.

In the timeless words of Machiavelli: *"Which respect (for the laws) was wise and good: none the less one ought never to allow an evil to run on out of regard for a good, when that good could easily be suppressed by that evil."*

Ten Myths of the Foolish and Feckless

Myth #10 - "Liberals love America like grown-ups" (Al Franken). George Bush is a cowboy who is out of his depth.

I do not doubt that most liberals sincerely love America. And many of them honestly believe what they are saying, even in the face of demonstrable evidence to the contrary. It's the grown-up part that rings hollow.

Grown-ups know how to exercise judgment. They know how to ask the right questions and come up with realistic solutions. They know how to think outside of the box, so to speak. George Bush has demonstrated all of these leadership qualities time after time. The foolish liberals can't see this because they are too busy still working out their problems with authority figures who say what they mean and mean what they say. In other words, liberals love America the way rebellious teenagers love their parents.

Franken makes a big deal of his statistics showing that Clinton outspent his predecessors on defense. He exults in turning the tables on Sean Hannity with figures uncovered by his fourteen diligent student researchers. "Bush can't lose with Clinton's military" Franken proudly proclaims.

Actually, according to the June 25, 2001 defense update of the National Priorities Project, "levels of spending on the Department of Defense decreased steadily in the late 1980s and all through the 1990s with the exception of 1999 and 2000. These decreases eventually brought spending back to the levels that existed before the Reagan build-up of the 1980s." So maybe Sean Hannity and Al Franken can both make respectable cases with their dueling statistics.

But Franken misses the larger point - the proverbial forest for the trees - that distinguishes sound judgment from sophistry. As Sean Hannity knows but Franken evidently does not, it is not just a question of whether Clinton gutted the military. The real question is whether he had the guts to use the military in the right way. So here is the larger point in bold type:

President Bush had the good sense and courage as Commander-in-Chief to use the military correctly and to maximum effect. He actually met with his intelligence heads on a regular basis, something Clinton neglected to do. The Bush Administration brought the disparate elements of "Clinton's military" together in a coherent plan that was brilliantly executed. Clinton had eight years to use his military the right way and stem the growth of terrorism but flubbed it. Did "Clinton's mili-

tary" do a great job in Afghanistan and Iraq? Yes. But it takes a good Commander-in-Chief to know how and when to use military force. Too bad Clinton lacked the judgment and courage to use it properly himself when he had the chance!

Lets take a look at another one of Al Franken's supposed "gotchas". Franken accuses Bush of lying when Bush claimed that during the Presidential campaign he would allow a deficit in the event of war. In Franken's words, "Bush never said anything remotely like it during the campaign." But actually he did do just that. He expressed his deficit views during the first New Hampshire Republican debate on January 7, 2000 moderated by Tim Russert:

> "If I ever commit troops, I'm going to do so with one thing in mind, and that's to win," Bush said.
>
> "And spend what it takes? Even if it means deficits?" asked the moderator, NBC's Tim Russert.
>
> "Absolutely," Bush replied, "if we go to war." (Source: AP, from Boston Globe)

Al Franken not only gets his facts wrong, but he misses the larger point. So once again, here it is in bold type:

President Bush has been true to his word. When he committed troops, he didn't rule out any option like his predecessor did in Kosovo, and he gave the troops all the support they needed to win.

Franken says "truth to power, baby" but he and his fellow liberals are afraid of a leader who is willing to confront the raw truth of the evil we face and to use the full power of the United States to defeat it. Foolish liberals need the security blanket of the United Nations even when there is nothing behind the blanket. They believe in what "should be" rather than deal with the world as it actually exists. Liberal believers cling to international law and institutions even when they are used to strangle us. They desperately want their country to do good - something all rational Americans share in common. But they equate decisive use of American strength in the service of our national interests as incompatible with doing good. History has proven otherwise right up to and including Iraq. It is time for the liberals to grow up.

The feckless French have a different problem. They have grown up, past their prime, into embittered cynics who put their self-interest above any moral principles. To the French, Bush is the proverbial cowboy - acting alone, shooting first and asking questions later. But of course that is at odds with the record of Bush's repeated attempts to reach an acceptable solution through the Security Council before he went ahead and followed through on his promise to enforce the Security Council resolutions along with Great Britain, Spain, Italy, the former Soviet satellites that are now proud and free nations of the "new" Europe, Japan, Australia and other allies. The French are so used to their own duplicity that they do not know how to deal with someone who talks and acts with conviction.

Take Chirac's preposterous doubletalk to Time Magazine:

"If Saddam Hussein would only vanish, it would without a doubt be the biggest favor he could do for his people and for the world. But we think this goal can be reached without starting a war."

If the French won't even interrupt their annual August vacation to rescue their elders from a horrendous heat wave - costing 10,000 lives during the summer of 2003 - how can we expect that they will sacrifice their parochial economic interests for a just cause in Iraq that is greater than themselves?

The French and liberals share a passion for talking a problem to death. The French couldn't deal with a plain-speaking Texan who wasn't taken in by their doubletalk.

France's designs for reclaiming its lost glory - and how President Bush's actions have gotten in their way - is worth its own chapter.

3

FRENCH FRUSTRATION

Chirac thought he had it all figured out. Only he didn't count on George W. Bush getting in his way.

Lets start with the Kyoto Protocol, that "noble" endeavor of Al Gore's to combat global warming by mandating the industrial nations to reduce their emissions to certain specified targets that varied by country or region. Al Gore's stupidity as a top U.S. negotiator offered Chirac a great opportunity to put the United States in its place.

Chirac played Al Gore perfectly. Chirac trumpeted the virtues of the Kyoto Protocol as a shining example of how world governance can save the ozone layer. But while Gore had his head in the clouds, Chirac was playing with the numbers.

Here's how the scam worked.

The environmental treaty set a target of reduction among industrialized nations in the commitment period 2008-2012 of at least 5 per cent below 1990 levels. The United States was given its own reduction target of 7%. The European Union agreed to a collective target of 8%, which the member countries could divvy up any way they wished.

France's reduction target - a big fat **zero**.

But that's not the worst of it. Chirac and his European buddies rigged the targets to suit themselves. It just so happens that Europe's emissions were high in 1990 and had been going down anyway from a high base. So it meant nothing for the Europeans to go back to 1990 as the baseline for measuring whether they met their commitments for future reductions. They could even increase their emissions once again from today's levels and still end up below the 1990 baseline by 2008 without breaking a sweat.

The United States already had relatively low carbon dioxide emissions in 1990. So an economy the size of the United States would necessarily take a big hit if we were to cut our emissions 7% below our 1990 levels.

A 1998 treaty ended up going back eight years as the baseline. The United Sates and Japan would have settled for some date in between. But the Europeans wanted no part of that. It was 1990 or no deal. Gore blinked first.

It's like playing a football game where one team has to move the ball 100 yards between goal posts for a touchdown, while the other team's offense only has to move a distance of fifty yards between the goal posts.

Scoring is a lot easier when you only have to go half the distance.

What's more, the EU under France's leadership blocked sensible alternatives such as allowing the United States to purchase permits from abroad where emissions can be reduced at a lower cost than in the United States. Without flexible international trading, the United States would be forced to curb its own greenhouse gas emissions by about 30 percent within 10 years. After you factor in population growth and increases in output, the gap between projected emissions and the Kyoto target will continue to grow.

Forest lands in the United States are net absorbers of carbon dioxide from the atmosphere. U.S. forest land absorbs about 270 million metric tons of carbon annually, equivalent to 17.1 percent of U.S. carbon dioxide emissions. Chirac blocked any compromise that would take this fact into account. He wanted the United States to reduce its economic growth enough to meet its full reduction target.

The global cost of the Kyoto Protocol has been estimated at $716 billion present value (as of 1999 when this estimate was made). The United States would bear almost two-thirds of the global cost *(Source: Requiem for Kyoto: An Economic Analysis of the Kyoto Protocol by Yale economics professor Dr. William D. Nordhaus and Joseph G. Boyer)*.

The United States would have to pay two thirds of the total cost, even though the United States produces 22 percent of the world's gross domestic product and accounts for no more than 25 percent of global emissions of carbon dioxide.

The hit to the U.S. economy of implementing the Kyoto Protocol? **Estimates show U.S. GDP losses averaging as high as 4.2% annually by 2010** *(Source: Energy Information Agency)*.

The hit to the French economy from implementing the Kyoto Protocol? Zero!

Chirac wants everyone in the world to have the right to emit carbon in equal amounts - with the United States suffering the worst penalties in real terms to compensate for a massive increase in the amount emitted by the developing countries like China and India who are not covered by the Kyoto Protocol.

> *"Each American emits three times more greenhouse gases than a Frenchman... France proposes that we set as our ultimate objective the convergence of per capita emissions."*

Never mind that annual carbon dioxide emissions per dollar of GDP in the United States have fallen by 15 percent since 1990. Or that, for example, in 1998 and 1999 U.S. greenhouse gas emissions grew by just one percent while the overall Gross Domestic Product grew by 8 percent. Efforts to increase energy efficiency and implement new technologies have begun to "de-link" economic growth and greenhouse gas emissions without having to shoot ourselves in the head.

Chirac's ultimate goal was not reduction of greenhouse gasses but reduction in U.S. strength. He meant to accomplish this through a web of international bureaucratic rules to tie the United States up in knots and restrain its growing economic power. For Chirac, the Kyoto Protocol would have been "the first component of an authentic global governance." Chirac says that he told George Bush he had to sign the Kyoto Protocol - "I told him there is no alternative to the signature and the adoption by the United States of the Kyoto accords."

The United States Senate had already rejected the treaty in principle by a vote of 95-0 during the Clinton Administration. Gore's mission to revive the treaty was a fool's errand that ended in failure. But true to form, Senator Kerry even back then blamed apathy in the United States and sympathized with other nations that "felt the U.S. was orchestrating a grand conspiracy against them". *(Speech at MIT, April 25, 1998 as reported in <u>The Tech</u>, April 28, 1998)*

Bush is a poker player. He saw the stacked deck the French wanted to play with and didn't fall for Chirac's Gallic charms.

While all this was happening, Chirac the environmentalist was playing Sheikh Iraq to Saddam to protect French oil interests. We have already discussed the corrupt bargain Chirac made with Saddam to ensure huge oil contracts for his friends at Elf.

With France's inside track to Iraq's vast oil reserves - second only to Saudi Arabia - Chirac knew that he would have a strong hand to price oil in euros instead of dollars. Chirac would be the undisputed leader of the EU if he could then position the euro as the world's reserve currency, a real body blow to U.S. economic power.

But Sheikh Iraq overplayed his hand. He called George Bush's bluff and lost. The result is that the United States now has reasonable access to Iraq's oil reserves. Iraq's oil infrastructure will be restored with American ingenuity, not French maneuvering. Iraq's oil production will increase, eventually approaching full capacity, priced in dollars rather than Euros.

Doing the right thing does pay off. But when you lie down with dogs, you get up with fleas.

So Chirac is furious that the "cowboy" President has frustrated his designs. He is obsessed with proving that France still matters in the world. He wants the United States to yield sovereignty over its own destiny so that France gets an equal say on the world stage.

> *"France wants to build a concert of nations in which its own national sovereignty is guaranteed and its right to pursue its national interests is recognized"* (Source: "The Geopolitics of France" (Stratfor Weekly) by Dr. George Friedman, a national security and intelligence expert who was founder and Director of the Center for Geopolitical Studies at Louisiana State University).

Chirac tries to manipulate world opinion and multilateral institutions to get a veto over what the United States can do to protect itself. Yet France takes no risk and commits nothing in the way of real sacrifice. It free-rides on U.S. military power and resolve. Chirac wants France to have the privileges of being a world power without any of the burdens and responsibilities.

But the jig is up, Monsieur Chirac a.k.a. Sheikh Iraq. You ran into a straight shooting President of the United States who has the guts to do the right thing whether it serves France's interests or not. And your arrogance has only served to diminish France's influence in the world, including the expanding Europe of free nations.

4

Pearl Harbor Redux

I woke up the other day in a cold sweat. I had the worst nightmare imaginable. It was December 7, 1941 and President Clinton was sitting in the Oval Office sharing a pizza with a girl named Monique who was laughing hysterically. Suddenly, Vice President Al Gore and Secretary of War Jimmy Carter came rushing into the room, and asked Monique to leave. Clinton looked rather annoyed as he fiddled with his fly. But the Vice President persisted.

> **Vice President Gore**: Mr. President, we have just received word that the Japanese have bombed our fleet at Pearl Harbor. We have lost more than 1400 men.
>
> **President Clinton**: I don't believe it. Where was our intelligence?
>
> **Jimmy Carter**: You told them to take the month off and come back after the holidays.
>
> **President Clinton**: But we have folks stationed all over the world trained to break code and communicate back to us by secure international phone lines. Gore, I put you in charge of that program. What happened?
>
> **Vice President Gore**: I know. I created what I call the "Intersnet" - short for International Spy Network. But we're still trying to work out some bugs.
>
> **President Clinton**: We were making such progress with the Japanese. All they needed was a little assurance and now they have gone and done this. Without even so much as a warning.
>
> **Jimmy Carter**: Never mind that. What are we going to do?

President Clinton: Assemble my Cabinet. But in the meantime, I want Al Franken right away.

Jimmy Carter: Franken? He's your political advisor. He doesn't know anything about military strategy.

President Clinton: Exactly. I need to know what will sell. You will take care of the military angle.

Al Franken enters the Oval Office and is given the grim news.

Franken: You need a bold response. Something that will get the American people's attention so that they know you mean business. I know. How about filling up a plane with Republicans and parachuting them into Tokyo with olive branches and rifles. The Japanese can choose which it is going to be.

President Clinton (laughing): That's good. But this needs to be bipartisan.

Franken: Seriously. I think the American people will be behind you whatever you do as long as you seem to be decisive.

President Clinton: We have to hit back.

Vice President Gore: You need to make some calls to our allies first. They hate surprises. And what about Hitler? Should we get his reaction? And what will the French think?

Jimmy Carter: Don't worry about Hitler. He's got his own problems and has no use for the Japanese. I was planning to go over to Germany soon anyway to help with their next election. I'll stop in Paris while I am in Europe.

Franken: Just ask Hitler what the French think. I'm sure he knows before they do.

President Clinton: We've got to compartmentalize this. The Japanese attacked us, not Germany. Lets focus on hitting Japan where it hurts. Any targets?

Jimmy Carter: We don't want to risk any innocent lives. How about one of Japan's uninhabited islands in the Pacific?

President Clinton: Not painful enough. It's the economy, stupid. Lets take out some of their factories - at night when nobody will be there to get hurt.

Vice President Gore: Not their auto factories. I've heard they are working on some fuel efficient cars that will use less gas and help save the environment. They don't have enough oil. That's why they attacked us in the first place - because we have cut them off from their oil supplies. Perhaps we can offer to work with them on building small cars and importing them here. Then they won't have a reason to fight and we'll be turning our attention together to fight global warming, the biggest threat to mankind.

President Clinton: What are you saying?

Vice President Gore: I'm saying that climate change is a more serious threat to the world than Emperor Hirohito and Hitler combined. Lets keep our priorities straight.

President Clinton: But we've got to respond forcibly to the attack on Pearl Harbor or we can kiss our re-election goodbye. Franken, am I right? Will the American people go along with just a stern warning to the Japanese not to do it again or they'll be sorry?

Al Franken: The Republicans will call us sissies.

President Clinton: Then we've got to win this.

Jimmy Carter: I've heard that they are using their camera factories as covers to make spy equipment and that they are experimenting with biological agents in their sushi. Lets go after that.

President Clinton: Alright. But lets act quickly. This has got to look tough. I need a strong speech to make before a joint session of Congress tomorrow night.

Vice President Gore: This would be an excellent time to declare war on global warming. And on the Japanese too if they don't change their ways and join us. I mean, we as a nation do share some of the blame here. There is little doubt that the way we currently relate to the environment is wildly inappropriate and that we are wasting oil that the Japanese desperately needed. But in order to change, we have to address some fundamental questions about our own purpose in life, our capacity to direct the powerful inner forces that have created this crisis, and who we are. Civilization and the earth are increasingly in conflict. The Japanese know this but are fighting the wrong battle. I think we can bring them around. If not, we'll…

Carter: If not, I'll be ready with a list of some camera factories and uninhabited islands and get our men ready to go after them.

Al Franken: So we turn the attack on Pearl Harbor into a call for global unity against global warming. We hit the Japanese with a symbolic reprisal to let them know we're not chopped teriyaki, but we sort of apologize at the same time to the world for wasting oil and ruining the environment. That will appeal to the hawks and the Greens at the same time!

President Clinton: OK. We've got a plan. Lets get to it.

The next thing I remember was the image of a plane hurtling into the Capitol Building and another into the Empire State Building - the kamikazie pilots had hit their marks and flashes of sprayed burning gasoline lit up the night. Screams of terror pierced the silence.

And then, thank God, I woke up. I remembered that President Franklin Roosevelt, a courageous Democrat, took the country to war against Japan and Germany right after the "day of infamy" and that he led the world to victory over the polluting evils of that time. I remembered his strength of purpose in confronting evil and one of his famous down-to-earth mottos: *"When you see a rattlesnake poised to strike, you do not wait until he has struck to crush him."*

And I remembered that we have a President today cut out of that same mold.

5

FINAL THOUGHTS

Some words of advice for the feckless and foolish.

To the French: Be true to your multilateral principles and give up your exclusive claim to a permanent seat on the Security Council. You never really deserved it in the first place and it is obvious to the world that you are even less worthy of it today. Instead, I suggest that you turn your seat over to the European Union and have it rotate among the membership (except for the United Kingdom, which will retain its own permanent seat). The new members from Central and Eastern Europe would share this rotating seat.

To Al Gore: You lost the Presidency fair and square under the rules set by our Constitution. Get over it. You now have the responsibility of the "wise statesman" who must measure his words carefully when offering his views. Be intellectually honest for once. Remember that you are an American before you are a Democrat or a "Move-on" liberal. Read some American history to get perspective on what prior Presidents have done in times of emergency before scaring people with Orwellian Big Brother bogeymen. Review your own past statements, and those of the President you served, about the grave threat posed by Saddam Hussein and the need to get rid of him one way or the other before you question George Bush's motives and integrity. In fact, take a look back at the transcripts of your debates with President Bush. You will find that Mr. Bush supported your Administration's actions in Kosovo and Iraq, saying only that he would deal more harshly with Saddam Hussein if he continued his defiance of the United Nations resolutions. Bush kept his word. Focus your intensity like a laser beam where it belongs - on the perpetrators of evil who mean this country harm, not on a President who is trying to do something about it.

And for goodness sake, stop whining about the Kyoto treaty. The U.S. Senate had already rejected it while you were in power and President Clinton did not try to re-submit it. The issue is not whether we need to address global warming in some fashion. The issue is how. You were taken to the cleaners in your negotiations - agreeing to a disproportionate cost burden on the United States that would have wrecked our economy for years to come. Admit it and "move on."

To Senator Kerry as the Democratic Candidate for President: By all means, attack President Bush on his policies if you must, but provide us with the why and wherefore of your own alternative vision. And don't demean yourself and the political discourse by resorting to angry accusatory rhetoric of your younger days. Bush is not the enemy. The fanatical terrorists and the dictators who help them are the enemies. They are the ones who committed real crimes against humanity. When you impugn the President's integrity in trying to deal with this threat and protect the American people the best way he knows how, you are giving the enemy an open invitation to strike again with impunity. By all means, disagree with the President on the wisdom of his decisions and question his claims of success. Present a detailed alternative strategy of your own and defend it. But don't use the megaphone that a Presidential campaign provides you to irresponsibly cannibalize this country's unity of purpose against our real enemies.

To Al Franken and Michael Moore: Continue to write your silly books, for all anybody cares. But don't pedal them as serious works. That's false advertising.

I end where this book began. We are living in a dangerous period of history when the nation's fragile freedoms are once again under attack by ruthless people who have no regard for life, much less liberty or the pursuit of happiness. Their delusions of grandeur feed on disunity, disorder and the weakness of others. Inaction breeds contempt and encourages bolder assaults - a painful lesson learned over the last decade and in the decades before World War II. But they cannot win when we pull together for the common good. Silence in the face of evil is not an option. Selfish obstructionism is the sure prescription for our freedom's fall from grace. I pray that the foolish and feckless see this in time to stop the fanatic terrorists before it is too late for all of us.

BIBLIOGRAPHY

Jane's Intelligence Digest and Jane's Foreign Report

Articles from:

    New York Times - *February 18, 2003, December 25, 2003, December 29, 2003, December 31, 2003, March 6, 2004*
    Arab News - *January 25, 2002*
    BBC News - *April 1, 2003*
    Concord Monitor - *December 26, 2003*
    Kurdistan Observer - *October 14, 2001*
    International Herald Tribune - *October 2, 2003*
    British Daily Telegraph - *April 28, 2003*
    Washington Post - *June 30, 2002*
    The Wall Street Journal Europe, *November 1, 2001*
    NewsMax.com, July 7, 2002
    The Guardian, *March 10, 2004*

The Privateers and the American Revolution, published online by PageWise, Inc

Requiem for Kyoto: An Economic Analysis of the Kyoto Protocol by Yale economics (Professor Dr. William D. Nordhaus and Joseph G. Boyer 1999).

The Geopolitics of France (Stratfor Weekly) by Dr. George Friedman

Bin Laden, Osama, *Jihad Against Jews and Crusaders World Islamic Front Statement* 23 February 1998

Bin Laden, Osama, *Declaration of War against the Americans Occupying the Land of the Two Holy Places* - published in Al Quds Al Arabi, a London-based newspaper, in August, 1996.

Fallaci, Criana, *The Rage and the Pride* (La Rabbia e l'Orgoglio 2002)

Franken, Al, *Lies and the Lying Liars Who Tell Them: A Fair and Balanced Look at the Right* (Dutton 2003)

Harris, Lee, *Civilization and Its Enemies: The Next Stage of History* (Free Press 2004)

Hitler, Adolf, *Mein Kampf* (1923-24)

Kundera, Milan, *Ignorance* (Perennial 2003)

Lewis, Bernard, *What Went Wrong?* (Perennial 2002)

Schama, Simon, *Citizens* (Alfred A. Knopf 1989)

United Nations Charter

Winston Churchill's Sinews of Peace Address, March 5, 1946 Westminster College, Fulton, Missouri

ABOUT THE AUTHOR

The author Joseph A. Klein is a practicing lawyer and Cum Laude graduate of Harvard Law School. He has written on a variety of public policy issues impacted by the law such as telecommunications, competition and privacy. This is Mr. Klein's first full-length book, where he uses his analytical skills to delve into the controversies swirling around the Bush Administration's approach to the war on terror, including its actions in Iraq, and to separate fact from hype.

ISBN 141202333-5